WHAT CAN YOU DO

Elizabeth –
a friend for more
years than we care
to count! Thanks for
being here –

What Can You Do

love,
Cynthia –

stories

Cynthia Flood

Cynthia Flood

A JOHN METCALF BOOK

BIBLIOASIS
WINDSOR, ONTARIO

FIRST EDITION

Library and Archives Canada Cataloguing in Publication

Flood, Cynthia, 1940-, author
    What can you do / Cynthia Flood.

Short stories.
Issued in print and electronic formats.
ISBN 978-1-77196-176-9 (softcover).--ISBN 978-1-77196-177-6 (ebook)

    I. Title.

PS8561.L64W33 2017   C813'.54   C2017-901947-3
                                          C2017-901948-1

Edited by John Metcalf
Copy-edited by Emily Donaldson
Cover designed by Gordon Robertson
Typeset by Chris Andrechek

Published with the generous assistance of the Canada Council for the Arts, which last year invested $153 million to bring the arts to Canadians throughout the country, and the financial support of the Government of Canada. Biblioasis also acknowledges the support of the Ontario Arts Council (OAC), an agency of the Government of Ontario, which last year funded 1,709 individual artists and 1,078 organizations in 204 communities across Ontario, for a total of $52.1 million, and the contribution of the Government of Ontario through the Ontario Book Publishing Tax Credit and the Ontario Media Development Corporation.

PRINTED AND BOUND IN CANADA

MIX
Paper from
responsible sources
www.fsc.org   FSC® C004071

To the new generation—
Lachlan, Gabriel, Shea, Rowan, Isis

Contents

WHAT CAN YOU DO

When we camped twelve years ago at Rosie's Park, the RVs took most of the sites, leaving for tents only some rough grass by the river. We four slept under canvas and woke to the sounds of moving water, of poplars trembling. Early in the morning a silent covey of quail crossed that green, to slip through a hedge to the meadow beyond. The plumed mother hustled her chicks along, speckled puffs.

Josh and Meghan still remembered those quail. Even at nineteen and twenty-three they'd imitate, giggling, the tiny scurry. They'd loved Rosie's raucous laugh, too, and her yard crowded with whirligigs—but this time our kids weren't with us.

When we parked by the hut marked *Office*, no Rosie. No one at all. Door locked, though the felt-board outside stated *Hours 9-7*. Some letters had shifted: *Sani ary dump fee, No oise after 10 p.* Rosie's plump figure, trotting about her property in capris and floral tee, didn't appear to call, "Havin' a good time, folks?"

Few cars. No other tents, so we'd have the greensward to ourselves. Most of the RVs now housed, we saw, not roamers but retirees. Solid furniture and bird-feeders stood under the metal awnings, near planters full of daisies, alyssum. Curtains—drawn.

A brindle dog, sole occupant of one gravelled site, slept in a cage beside a cook-stand with a portable barbecue atop, padlocked.

"Where is everyone?"

"Nap-time?" My husband guessed.

The river ran fast.

"Isn't it higher than before?"

"Mmm. Mosquitoes maybe," he said. "After supper let's walk to the village. Remember that store? The bridge?"

"You want candy."

He smiled. "You like antiques."

"So-called."

The dog rose clumsily off his haunches, nosed at the chain-link.

"A bad limp, friend." My husband fondled the soft stripy ears.

I did too. "Was he here, before?"

"Dunno."

We brought the car close to the river, got our chairs and books and iced tea, found poplar shade.

Dozing, I breathed menthol.

A nasal voice said, "Rosie's gone away. I'm Dearie.'"

My eyes opened to a thin old child. No, woman.

Lines scored her face. Cigarette in hand. Worn cut-offs. Flip-flops. A shabby tank. Grey roots, split blonde ends. Bandages round bony ankles, one strapped with a small black oblong.

"Yeah, Dearie. Tents, fifteen. Just the one night? Got cash?"

Exhaling, she folded the bills in with her Cameos. Pointed out stand-pipe, washrooms, trash cans, the high river.

"Rosie's all upset about mosquitoes. She's got me foggin, foggin, yesterday, s'morning, tomorrow. Takes me hours."

If we hadn't that day driven three hundred miles in our steel box, if we hadn't sat down to read, chosen our tent-site, we'd have decamped to another brief home. Instead my husband changed the subject, his strategy for avoiding difficult moments.

"Sorry not to see Rosie. We stayed here years ago, with our kids, and she was a lot of fun."

"Oh she can be that, *mother*-in-law." Pause. "But *she's* not here. S'all up to me. Trash, the damn residents, the town goin on about back taxes. And *he* don't do much."

My strategy is to ask questions, but Dearie left before I chose one.

We set up tent and stove, fetched water.

"Dearie, how old?"

He made a *Dunno* face. "Forty maybe."

"That skin, the awful hair! Fifty at least."

"Could be."

We zipped the sleeping-bags together, then ate our meal, with river and trees as dinner music.

Before our walk, we locked the car.

In the women's room, a sign by each lethargic toilet read *Hold lever down 'til clear. Think of others!* Rosie's curly script appeared again by the tampon machine's broken coin slot, *Ladie's Supplies at Desk.* The shower curtain crackled with scum. I sighed. The night before we'd camped at a forestry site, the sole amenity a pit toilet.

En route to the village's tiny business area, we walked by peach trees, plums, apples, their branches loaded with June's hard green. Morning glory, wild rose wreathed the hedges. Kids and dogs ran everywhere.

The store's bell jangled us in. Still that pyramid of junk food—years ago, how our children gasped!

No shoppers, no one at the cash register. We browsed the aisles of furniture, mirrors, indeterminate objects treasured once, resented now. Last time we'd happily bought an old citrus-juicer, heavy green glass.

"Wouldn't Josh love this oak desk?"

"Maybe too big for the car?"

"I was just imagining him. Sitting there."

He sighed. "I imagine nice things too."

Seeing no price tag, we moved on to treats, and a tired woman emerged from the back as we neared the till.

"That oak desk?"

"Seven hundred."

"Wow," he said.

"Yeah. I keep telling the owner he over-prices, and then he complains stuff don't sell. You at Rosie's?" She rang up our purchases. "That fog floats uphill. Stinks. We gotta close our windows. She won't listen. Well. What can you do." On *do,* her voice sank.

The door jingled us out, and we found the little bridge.

No cars, bikes, pedestrians. Again we admired the line of hills, distant beyond the river's glitter that vanished round a curve. Poplars and willows dipped into the blue-brown green, while half-submerged bushes waved as if struggling to get out. We leaned on the rail, eating sweet. Dragon flies and water boatmen sparkled.

Standing close, I wanted to touch him. We hadn't, in months.

Swallows darted dipped swerved.

Instead I asked him if he thought Dearie's tracker had scraped her ankles, admitting infection? Or—just sensitive skin? Why house arrest? Why not wear a concealing runner-and-sock combo? To offer the world a general *Fuck you?*

When we'd gutted these topics I stupidly asked aloud what I'd so often asked myself, on this, our first escape in a year.

"What do you think we'll find at home?"

He took my hand. "I keep remembering this morning. Those kids. The boy."

At a cafe in a coastal town we'd stopped for coffee.

Newspapers, board games lay on a shelf. A boy and a younger girl drank smoothies and played chess, watched by a big brother? Cousin? He had golden curls.

My big-city paper featured, in *Living Today*, photos of a rose show just opening. Such colours! Perhaps we could...

My husband said, "Oh no."

He'd chosen the town's tabloid. Page One: a boy's grad photo topped *18-Year-Old Drowns/Dad Saved/Near Harbour.*

I read the standard tale: change in weather, huge wave, boat overturned, life jackets MIA, yada yada.

"How could they be so stupid?"

He looked puzzled. "It isn't that simple."

"Why not?"

"Not if you've lived by water all your life."

"What excuse is that?"

He shrugged.

In the capsize, the fisherman dad broke his arm. Neither he nor the boy's best pal, along for the celebratory trip, could find him sunk where tidal waters slammed up against fresh. The friend hauled the father to land.

The young girl held a pawn, thinking.

I finished reading about roses. "You don't want to discuss this, do you?"

He hesitated. "Sometimes I wonder what people say about us, Josh's parents."

"What do they know?"

"Well." He spooned up sweet foam. "I'm not a hundred percent sure we've always done the right things."

"Didn't we get him into treatment? Isn't it up to him now?"

"As I said before." He saw the roses I'd been looking at, smiled. "You'd like to see that show, on the way back?"

The chess-watcher's curls shook with sudden laughter. He clapped. The girl blushed. The boy pouted, then applauded. Off they all went, into their bright day.

I visited the women's room. So shiny.

Back in the car, he said, "Next stop, Rosie's!"

His cheerful turn to drive. Just as well. Make-up's a flimsy shield.

As we walked then from the bridge towards the RV park, I remembered that the kids and I had met a pretty cat. Kittens too. I slowed.

"No thanks."

He went on, and I wandered alone past yards brimful of the syrupy summer light. Everywhere Josh and Meghan giggled, pointed, exclaimed. Seven, eleven.

"Mum, can't we take the little calico home?"

"She's too young, dear." Tears strove to exit.

At the Park, a big pick-up was pulling in. The driver and I nodded as the brindle dog struggled up, barking his delight.

I saw my husband, near a utility shed, by a man wearing a straw hat with a black band. Suddenly this man bent over a trash bag, bent as if he'd collapse without that bulk. Two, three seconds. Not touching my husband's proffered hand, he straightened. Saw me. Tipped his gondolier's hat. Bald. And turned away.

My husband said quietly, "Just helping Warren with the trash."

We headed for our tent-home, but as we passed the truck driver's site he opened the dog's cage. Nothing for it but to stop. Greet. Chat. Pat.

The brindle sniffed me, wagged.

"Good boy!"

"Old boy?" asked my husband.

Ralph nodded. "Had him nine years. Found him. Side of the highway, left to die. Figured him then for five, six."

He threw a red ball.

The men spoke of the tools and machinery in the pickup's box, of local farming practices. I drifted towards our site. The limping dog ran, retrieved, ran. At last Ralph lit his barbecue, and my husband rejoined me.

"How could you talk so long? Who's the guy in the hat?"

"Warren. Wait."

He fetched a map from our car, then sat down hard, by me. "That boy? In the paper? Who drowned? Rosie's at his funeral."

Oh awful, awful as could be.

An only child. Rosie's sole grandchild.

Gondolier Warren, Rosie's other son: uncle to the dead. Dearie's husband. *So he couldn't go because of her,* I almost said, and almost *Good they don't have kids.*

"Why didn't the cashier tell us?"

Surprised, "We're strangers."

Stupid me.

Unfolding the map, he pointed at a blue wriggle. "That cafe? This same river. The boy spent summers here. Threw that ball. That's why no one's around."

"Stop."

He wiped his eyes.

Side by side, quiet, quiet, we imagined how, after such an event, no one can, at first, bear to tell those who must know. We twitched, frantic to hear Josh speak and to ask

Meghan about her brother, but we'd all three sworn to phone only in emergency.

Which, he and I agreed, this wasn't. Already in that coastal town the mourning flowers coloured the grave, or had been given away, tossed out.

From the barbecue rose the smell of wieners.

The dog slowed.

"Ralph sleeps in his truck?"

He nodded. "Day labour on farms round here. Repairs, servicing."

Dusk came on.

My husband got wine from the cooler, twisted off the cap. "Probably those two made a fine couple once. Pretty little blonde, tall dark etcetera."

Bewildered. "You mean Dearie?"

"You didn't see Warren close up. Handsome, once," pouring. "Rosie's lost her marbles. He's trying to run the place." He sipped. "Any kittens?"

"No."

The campfire we'd planned felt too public, happy. Instead, while darkness thickened we drank and ate and offered silent witness as the birds concluded their testimony. Stars appeared, bats flickered by. No mosquitoes.

Crawling into our tent, I inhaled stale menthol.

Our pillows and books lay differently.

We searched. The tent pocket where he'd stashed his All-Sorts—empty. He smiled. "You don't like that liquorice smell anyway."

True. Not the point, but after twenty-seven years we sometimes recognize what's not worth discussing.

Into bed. Quiet. No reading. Air moved through our flimsy home into the quivering poplars. Invisible, the river rushed to tide water. I did not ask if my husband thought Dearie was sucking his candy. If she and Warren shared a bed. If she changed her dressings, slipped a lacy nightgown over her bones, took her tracker off.

He slept.

Stupid me. We should have bought that desk. Too late. We should never have left home. My fault. Warren hairless, the dog old, like failing Rosie, like us. What can you do. I counted, counted his soothing breaths.

At dawn, amid wild birdsong I woke and went out to pee.

The dog's tail twitched. Wieners hissed on the barbecue as Ralph's long day began.

A flutter in the grass.

I stood still.

My husband was awake too, peering from our tent as the tiny speckled puffs floated through the hedge. When the mother quail's plume vanished, I got back into our sleeping bag and we grabbed each other, sour mouths, unwashed bodies, bristle-chin, the works.

Then we left the sorrowful Park, aiming for the house that, as far as we knew, still held our darlings.

GOING OUT

You've broken up after five years, no record-breaker but not a fling either, and you're learning how much your single lives resembled each other inside that shared life, because everywhere you go (except for thirty-five hours of weekly work, thank heaven) there he is. And again *It's over*.

You opt out of the film series. Out of the hiking group, so you don't witness those trees on the high autumn trails, blazing up just before they go, and you stay away from the specialty wine shop—but he too must be avoiding restaurants you once frequented, for there he is, again, gobbling paella at the new Spanish place in Kitsilano (you both despised trendy Kits), and days later it's salmon benny at the Sylvia (so dull).

Like you, he's smoking again, a "friend" says.

The sympathy offered a dumped woman—you've charted its tight limits. He's not dead is he? Indeed no, still pals with his pals, some of whom live with or are even married to yours. This social circle includes actual widows, but when they moan, people don't change the subject. They attempt comfort. These same people find it "hard" now to plan parties, apologize for not inviting you, how about Thanksgiving? A month away.

When you buy a ticket to a fundraiser for refugees, you know he'll attend, also much mutual acquaintance—but you can't hide at home reading mysteries forever. Can you? The cat's warm on your lap. Too warm. Push her off, go out, face the world, socialize. Your book club's taken a table for the event. Perfect.

Imperfect: a full parking lot and a search along dark rainy streets, blocks from the hall. As you walk back to the bright windows (damp skirt clutching your knees), you smoke because the place is likely non-smoking. In you go.

Perfect, you're right, no cigarettes till you head home. External control. Here's your club's table. *Late, yes, sorry, yes!* Smiles waves kisses hellos.

Imperfect: flu has kept one member from this sold-out event. Beside the only available chair sits an unknown old man.

Deal with this, seat yourself—and at once you confront the vision, five tables away, of your ex's profile. His affectionate smile. You can't nor do you wish to see the woman it's aimed at, so you turn left, but this member, tedious anyway, has turned thus also for a chat. So you turn right.

The old man inspects the printed program through thick glasses. One hand grips card stock, the other forefinger slides down the text. Fingernails ridged like celery, knuckles knobbed, no wedding ring. So old. Bent, hunched. He smiles. At funny refugees?

He's set down his glasses case on a worn paperback. You wish its spine faced you. You wish you'd brought a book yourself, to get you through. In the women's room you'd fly away with Warshawski, even Morse. How old's this solitary, anyway? Eighty?

You and your ex did exchange rings in a giggly champagne-y way, on a moonlit beach in Tofino. Recently you threw yours at him. Your cat chased it under a bookcase. Later, the circle tinkled into your building's metals/plastics recycling bin.

Now the old man smiles. He says his name, proffers a little writing pad. What? Oh. You're to print your name, because he's deaf. Stone deaf. Can't lipread. (Towards the end you asked more than once *Have you gone deaf?*) This one has a clear voice, low. Not quite something, normal?

You write, *Do you work with refugees?*

"Oh no," cheerfully. "When you're old and live alone, events like this are refreshing. So many people. Much better than TV."

Pathos. How to respond?

I see you are a reader, too.

Good, he smiles again, takes up the volume: *Who Travels Alone: An Oswald Fisher Mystery*. Much read. Thickened. Wrinkly as he.

You're a fan?

"I've read all the Fishers, reread 'em. The first chapters of this"—many pages flip by under his thumb—"maybe a dozen times."

Why on earth reread a mystery?

What's it about?

He hesitates. Pokes at the pad. "So limited. Could I—just *tell* you? It'd get us through, till the speaker starts."

You're horrified, then not. Perfect! You needn't risk glimpsing your ex or her. You needn't endure your leftward neighbour, who admits to reading the ends of mysteries first so as to "enjoy" stories sucked dry of all suspense.

Here come the servers, plates loaded. You reach for the table's wine, pour, touch rims with the old man, smile into his warm brown eyes.

Slowly he tells.

In an expensive hotel restaurant a couple dine, observed by Oswald Fisher (always observant) from a nearby table. Smiling, she prattles until her prawn cocktail arrives. Her make-up Fisher deems successful; the face could pass for fifty. Her figure, no. She's encased, armoured. Fisher drops some factoids about what shape-wear does to the digestive organs.

You assess this old man's tone—pleased? Scornful? But fifty's not old.

The woman, smiling under pink lamplight, fingers her glittering gift, a necklace. Steaks arrive. The two eat. Their dessert's meringue-y. Fisher grimaces.

Aha! You recognize a Manly Sleuth who dislikes sugar, cats, fiction. Doubtless he knows all about some war. You roll your eyes. No one rolls back.

The old man describes how the waiter takes a photo of the loving pair, and the husband grins. "Darling, another surprise! In the car. I'll get it."

Lights shine down on his baldness as he goes. The wife fingers up the last sweet smears and looks about, savouring, waiting.

He doesn't come back. He doesn't. *Doesn't!*

A giggle resonates inside the teller's voice.

Soon waiter, hostess, manager, concierge move into action and report. Fisher witnesses, discreetly like all great detectives. The car's gone from the hotel's parkade. The husband's gone. Police appear, search. Yes, they declare, he's gone. The reluctant wife pays the bill. Then she too must go, in a taxi.

"All alone!" As the old man laughs openly, his dentures click.

You set down your fork on hearing those two sounds.

Absent any conscious decision, you take your purse and rise.

As you move towards wherever you're going you buy raffle tickets (angry fingers struggle to open your wallet). Also you inspect the goods on offer in the silent auction. Nothing appeals. People smile at you, people wave, so you head out of the dining hall and downstairs to the exit.

The first inhale: the best, always. Oh god you've missed this so.

Coatless, you welcome the chill dark. Some lights glare down on the wet parking lot. Other solitary smokers, unknown, make red dots that fade, brighten.

So quiet. Your anger lessens. An old jerk who's refused to learn lip-reading, why make him important? Irrelevant. A lump on the next chair. Actually you could just go home, right now—but for sure some reader-pal, ever thoughtful, would collect your coat, and she'd think *Poor you*. So, no.

Your cigarette spits in a puddle. Pack and lighter dive into your skirt's pocket, at the ready.

During your absence the hall's got very warm. A line-up overwhelms the bar, noise swells, people block the spaces between tables.

The old man's hunched over Fisher. "Hello there! Thought maybe you'd got mad." Gleeful, yes.

On his pad you print *Why do you laugh at her?*

He frowns. Looks at you. His eyes—they're grey, cold, like the Pacific that windy night.

You pour more wine, none for him, and listen.

Later the police find the husband's car, driven off-road into a rampart of blackberry bushes in a park. No one inside. No clue. Search routines unfold at airports, train stations, car rentals. The wife cries, hands over his passport and whatever else the police want. Business associates act like her, minus the tears.

You empty your glass, grab the pad. *Why does he leave?*

Startled, "Of course because he hates her!"

For six months, no news. Then police in another city (Fisher's there too, conveniently) discover a bald corpse in a hotel elevator.

Your eyebrows go up.

Irritably, "Yes, there's twists, turns, more murders, but that opening's the best. Such a public fool that woman makes of herself!"

Rage rises like vomit.

Up again, this time to the washroom.

En route you try to take long, slow breaths, and suc-
ceed. You continue breathing thus on the toilet, as you
contemplate men's infinite capacity to exploit the infinite
kindness of weak women.

When you face the washroom's gigantic mirror, you're
surprised that your hair doesn't resemble a fright wig or
writhe like Medusa's. You use comb, lipstick, and run cold
water over your wrists. Run run, cold colder.

Two other women join you. One's decades before
fifty, the other's way past, and the triple image makes you
say, "Shit!"

"That bad?"

"Yes," you answer the older woman. "Right now it is."

The younger one, anxious, scurries out.

"Nothing lasts."

You don't say, "Thanks for nothing."

Back to the crowded hall.

Where's that young woman? Is she ——? No. At a table
far from your ex's, she's kissing a man much younger than
he. A warmth, something, pulses through you and away.

Near your table, you meet your boring neighbour,
fresh drink in hand. She whispers, "Have you heard?"

"What?"

That the absent club member's flu is fictional, her time
nearly up. Your cold hands twist.

"So young!" sighs the bore.

Untrue. Anger swells, swells higher when, at your
table, you see an empty chair. Where the hell has he gone?
You have to deal with him... but now the exec director,

important, self-deprecating, arrives at the dais to introduce the event's honoured guest.

Applause.

This person duly speaks, speaks.

The drone soon fades out, for you are hovering
outside the men's room to ask strangers, "Is an old man
in there?"

You check the bar, the raffle table.

Weapon in hand, you head downstairs and out. A taxi's
pulling up, and the old man's carrying his book. Perfect!

You grab *Who Travels Alone*, click your lighter, start
burning and screaming.

Other people appear.

He laughs and laughs.

You shout and shove at him, shove hard, harder.

He falls, hits his head on the taxi. His glasses shatter.
More witnesses gather, incredulous, including your ex,
cigarette in hand, bewildered, now running away like a
refugee, with her, over fifty for sure, and as you kick and
burn and cry, your own dear book-pals arrive on scene.
They've brought your coat.

DOG AND SHEEP

Late in the afternoon the dog appeared again, around a
curve some way ahead on the road.

She had often come trotting back to us, for we were
slow, halting often to name and photograph a flower, or
to query as our tour guide spoke of local limestone for-
mations. Of French cheese-making. Of the peasant houses
(animals downstairs, people up) in the Cathar villages
we'd visited. Of the Cathar heresy, whose adherents saw
evil and good as equal powers, chose poverty, strove to
be kind. Of their betrayers, informants paid in the usual
currencies of cash or sex.

"Shocking," we agreed.

French wine-making, too. *Terroir*, very important.

Nearer the dog came, wagging, closer, until those at
the front of our walking group cried out. Others halted.
In a huddle, we all stared.

Blood covered the dog's muzzle, stained the delicate
fur beneath her eyes, dabbled an ear.

"My God, what's she done?"

"Horrible!"

Our cries drove her off a little, puzzled, tail drooping. Through that red mask she peered at us over her shoulder.

Early that morning, this dog had turned up.

As we left the *gite* where we'd spent the night, we'd spoken of the Inquisition's unsparing work in that particular village. In 1308 every single resident got arrested for heresy.

Our walking tour itself was titled *In The Footsteps of the Cathars*, though most participants had signed up to see the beautiful Pyrenean foothills. Some did feel that faith, if not extreme, might sustain social order? In a good way? One or two, confusing Cathar with Camino, had expected to follow a specific route taken by all the heretics to a singular destination.

"I wonder how many Cathars, total, got burned at the stake."

"Are we going to be so gloomy all day?"

"I'm just glad I didn't live then."

"Tomorrow's the castle of the Really Big Burn."

"Oh no, not rain again!"

At the last house in the village, our guide paused till we all caught up. "Our way starts here."

A single gravestone stood at a field's edge, tilting somewhat and obscured by long, wet grass. *Ici est morte*, we read in our sketchily-remembered high-school French. *Ici est morte / 18 Août 1944 / Castella Pierre / innocente victime / de la barbarie Nazie.*

"Glad I wasn't here for that, either."

Then this dog rose out of a ditch.

A mutt. Thin, scruffy, brown, collar-less, small-eyed. Long, dark nipples swinging. She came close, wouldn't quite allow pats, whimpered, scuttled away, returned to circle and sniff, hung back till she saw where we tended. Then she rushed ahead to wait for us, panting.

"D'you suppose she has puppies somewhere near?"

"Get away!" Our guide thrust his hazel stick at her. She yelped.

"If so, she'll go back to the village," we concluded, going on.

As we were led from one thin grassy path to another, then to a narrow road of beaten earth, light rain continued. The breeze wafted moisture at us, swirled it into loose airy necklaces. On all sides the fields spread out in spring green, shining wet, while in the distance the terrain sloped up, dotted with sheep, to a forested plateau.

"Up there we shall walk," our guide said.

The dog trotted ahead, looking back to check we were still in view.

Behind us sounded a—truck? French. So little! We smiled, moving aside for the vehicle to pass, but it stopped so the three men inside could joke and talk with our guide. They spoke fast. We grasped nothing.

The driver pointed inquiringly at the dog.

"*Problème.*" Our guide shrugged.

More laughter. As the van moved off, the unknown men wiggled their eyebrows at us and waved.

"Foresters," said our guide. "They work near where we walk today. Remove the rotten branch. Inspect for pasts, no, pests."

"How on earth do they manage with that van? *Trop petite!*"

"Earth? Manage?"

The discussion lasted until we neared a larger road. In its middle sat the dog, her head sticking up above the hedge lining the route. She watched us.

"Thinks she's hiding."

"Stupid! She'll get run over. Why the hell doesn't she go back where she came from?""

"Never been trained."

Our guide chased her until she howled and ran off.

"Good!"

We crossed the road and walked alongside a field. Its unknown tall grains swayed close by us, their wet, silky heads making moiré patterns under the breeze. Mesmerizing.

Without notice, our guide turned into a tall green tunnel of shrubs and small trees, a boreen running off at an angle from the field. We'd not noticed the entrance, draped with wet vines.

"Just as well this isn't a self-guided tour!"

"Too right, we'd be lost in no time."

After emerging from the tunnel, we started uphill. Half an hour later we looked back at the valley, a long trough full of silver-green air resembling the great stone troughs in the villages we'd passed through, now empty shapes, once full, sparkling with laundry and the hands of women.

Now we ascended a great staircase, once terraced farmland, the steps blurred by disuse to faint ledges. The rain got serious. We stopped to put on rain pants and jackets, then continued.

After an hour the dog reappeared, wagging madly. Someone reached out to pat. She snapped, cringed, ran.

"Damn that bitch!"

"Maybe her puppies got taken too early, and she's upset."

"Can't we get her back to where we started?"

"You're kidding, right?"

Our dour guide moved on. The temperature dropped steadily, the rain chilled. As hands sought gloves and woolly hats, the dog came near again. She'd stretch out her front paws and drop her head, abasing herself, then look up in hope.

"No! Nothing for you."

We climbed. She came close, sniffed, almost nudged.

"Go home!" Whack of the hazel stick.

She yelped, but stuck around.

When at last we attained the forested plateau, the dog pranced about and shook herself as if happy to be in the dry. So were we. All wrong. Up there, a freshening wind blew rain through the trees and made their foliage shed thousands of cold drops already accumulated.

Our way was stony, muddy, and so narrow that the dog left the track to move among the trees. Some of us tried that too, but low branches and hidden roots made our balance as uncertain as did the stones underfoot. Stepped on, they often slid. We stepped in liquid mud, stepped, stepped among the black pines sheathed in ebony plates. Sweet-smelling fir. The thin grey trunks of *fagus sylvatica*. Holm oaks, festooned with catkins.

"Where's that dog got to?"

"Who cares? Headed back to the village, probably."

"Sensible creature's gone to shelter. Not like us!"

Everyone laughed, except our guide.

"A dog to run about the forest is not good. Higher up on the *montaigne,* wild boar. Deer. Sheep of course. And—wolfs?"

"Wolves."

We went on.

Were those animals watching as we came through their country? Some in our group had seen wild boars on YouTube. Not as large as pigs. Mean tusks, though. One told a story from a TV newscast about a huge sow in Ontario stomping on a drunk, killing him.

A howl sounded from behind, a blundering rush. We turned. Just as the frantic dog reached us, we sensed a blurred motion away, away in the trees—and gone, like a curtain shaken then still.

"Roe deer," said our guide. "Bad animal!" He shook his stick.

The dog's chest heaved. Whining, she skulked off, followed again.

Then the terrain altered. Plateau, *fini.* We started down.

Steepness—odd, to be almost vertical after two hours' walking on the flat! Our feet felt unfamiliar. Trees changed: more conifers, fewer deciduous. *Progress*, we thought. Also we wondered, *Lunch?* Daily, leaving our *gîtes*, we each got ten inches of buttered baguette (we measured) stuffed with meat or fish, plus hard-boiled egg and tomato. Local cheese, a slab. Cold meat, sliced. Fresh salad. Cake. Our guide carried dark chocolate, also a mini camp stove for hot drinks.

We went on.

The rainy twist of trail down through the trees grew steeper. We slowed. The stones now underfoot were larger than those up on the plateau, but they still slipped. Terracotta-coloured mud ran two inches thick, clogging our boots. Our hiking poles became essential for every step, while our guide moved urgently amongst us to point out safe foot placements, repeat *Attention!* Rain fell. Some of us did too, delaying the group to cope with minor injuries.

We murmured of forestry campsites at home, of fire-watchers' cabins. Did our guide plan a lunch-stop at a similar place?

That dog came close again, but at every reaching hand she'd show her teeth. Shouts and rushes drove her off, snarling.

Watch! Attention!

Always the path turned down through the pines to— where? None of us knew. With so many conifers, the forest's ambience dulled. No more wry jokes about *la boue*. Silence, except curses and rain.

Again the dog. On her forelegs, mud reached above the carpal pad.

"Poor thing!"

"Poor thing bit me, remember?"

"She needs people."

"We don't need her."

Another distant noise sounded, *r-rr-rrrrrr*. Not animal. Mechanical, piercing. It'd hurt your ears, close up. *Rrr-r-r-r-r.*

"Must be the foresters."

"Why haven't we seen them?" What route did they take? Surely that cartoon vehicle couldn't go cross-country like an ATV?

Then our guide loosened his pack. "Time to eat."

Here? Steep slope. Dripping pines. No stumps or rocks to sit on. In a ring of soggy backpacks on the forest floor, we ate standing up.

R-rr-rrrr, further off.

The dog grovelled, whined, begged. Our guide, about to shoo her, aborted his gesture when one of us tossed a slice of ham. Another threw torn bits of baguette. A tomato landed on the mud, a cube of cheese.

Even as the dog swallowed, her pleading glance came again.

"*C'est tout!*" Our guide raised his voice.

"No more, greedy girl."

Some of us ate everything, some repacked a lot. We stretched, or leaned against trees to relax while drinking coffee and tea, well-sugared. The dog sidled amongst us, sniffing at hands, bums, packs.

"Are you deaf? That's *all!*"

Packs on again, poles in hand, *la boue* again.

Down those stony steeps for another nameless time, down, down. More slips, wrenches, bruises. Only the chill rain stayed steady, and the dog slinking off into the trees (who cared what kinds they were?) or weaving amongst us on her muddy paws. Once, near the trail, she squatted.

"Dammit, not here!"

Small dry turds.

How far, how much longer? Some asked, others cringed. Like kids pestering a parent, we knew what our guide would say.

The rain ceased. Unnoticed, briefly. At ten that morning we'd reached the plateau; our watches said five p.m. when we realized that the sound of falling water was MIA.

The steep softened first into a hill, next to a slope. The dog lolloped ahead, out of sight. In bright sunshine, peeling off sodden jackets and hats and gloves, we exited the forest, laughing.

Finally our guide smiled. "Now we see the Kermes oak. Not the holm any more."

Our legs, trembling, sought to adjust as we moved into the valley and across a sunny meadow sprinkled with primula, tricolour pansy, anemone, cowslip, speedwell, all bright-eyed still with rain.

The Pyrenean foothills rose ahead, one crowned with grey ruined teeth, the castle where the greatest immolation occurred. To be bundled alive into fire or to deny their faith: two choices, those Cathars had.

We walked alongside a brook whose current carried a thousand spangles downstream, and reached a gravel road. This, our guide assured us, led to the nearby town where we would spend the night.

Round a curve ahead, the dog appeared again. Came closer, trotting, wagging. Those at the front of our group stopped.

We all stopped.

"Look, horrible!"

"Awful!"

"What's she done?"

Over her shoulder, that puzzled red face, peering.

We hastened forward.

In a depression at the roadside lay a large ewe, fallen.

She nearly resembled an illustration for a children's book, that sheep. Background: blue sky, tall green grass. Foreground: a beautiful creature in her seemingly restful motherly pose, in her roundness, her billowy shining creamy woolliness—but her hindquarters, fully exposed to our view, had been savaged to a bloody mangle. One leg was raw. She could not move.

Patient, full of pain, her large eyes met our gaze.

"Wolf," stated our guide.

"Not—?"

"Her? No no, too stupid, she just sticks in her nose for a taste. Wolf." He pointed up to the steeps we'd just descended.

Some loudly wished for a gun, a knife. Others noted that the sheep was not ours to kill. We walked on along the valley.

The brook, still shallow, grew broader. While fording it, by silent agreement we lured with ham the red-faced dog who'd chosen us. We grabbed her, struggling; we splashed and rubbed her furry yelping face till she no longer looked a murderer. Controlling her thus, we touched her nipples. Hard as horn. No loved puppies, not for years.

At the first farm we reached, our guide went in to leave word of the desperate sheep, so that her owner in this life could be notified and come to end his property's pain.

"They will phone him," he said, returning.

Would this happen before the wolf came back?

We went on. The dog circled near, ran off, came back. No one threw food. No one tried to pat.

Why, we asked ourselves, did this animal, so obviously fearing yet desiring human contact, not have a home?

Did the SPCA operate in France? Even if so, there'd hardly be a branch in the small town.

Why are people so careless?

Why do they not train their dogs?

Why do they not affix identification tags to their dogs' collars, vaccinate the animals, have their teeth checked?

What could we do about the damn dog?

"*La mairie*," said our guide when we put the matter to him. "We'll take her there."

The town hall was closed, though, by the time we'd walked over the centuries-old bridge (our stream had grown to a river) and threaded our way along the narrow streets, faced with houses washed in white or cream, to the green of the central square. Here stood rubbish bins where we dumped our leftovers, and there a fountain played near a memorial listing locals killed in centuries of wars. A smaller, special stone was dedicated to local *héros de la résistance*. The plane trees' dappled trunks were re-dappled by the late sun among the leaves, and, on one corner of the square, red shutters shielded the windows of our small hotel.

Exhaustion, held back for hours, poured into us. As we entered the lobby, the dog pushed forward too.

"*Mais non*," said Monsieur to the animal that had walked twenty kilometers with us that day. (Thirty, given how she'd run back and forth and circled?) The door, closing, touched her nose.

Later we sat in a pleasant sitting room looking out through small panes to the hotel's courtyard, bright with red pelargoniums. A fire warmed the hearth. Madame, smiling, poured *kir* for us and for guests from other tours. Quite a United Nations we made, really, travellers from every continent.

And here were the foresters again. One exclaimed, "You made so loud noise!" All three laughed. Graceless, we felt. Dumb tourists, trailed unawares by savvy locals.

Another forester chortled, "We found this." A glove, with a clip for attaching to a belt. "Not latched, no good! And this." A candy wrapper.

Barbarians.

The third commented, "That dog with you, we see her often today. No good in the woods. No sense."

"*Ouaf ouaf*, all the time!" agreed Monsieur. "I have let her stay there," and he pointed to the courtyard, "tonight. Then she goes out."

A wicker chair by a puddle offered partial shelter from the rain. Nose on paws, the bitch looked up.

"Out where?"

Monsieur made the face that says *Not my concern*. No, his busy schedule wouldn't feature escorting a stray to the town hall. As for Madame, her mien indicated complete abstention from this topic.

"Couldn't we——?"

Our guide answered, "We leave too early."

After a jagged silence, one forester suggested that he

and his fellows return the dog to the village we'd walked from, that day.

"We work there tomorrow. It is her home, yes?"

Who knew?

The glove's owner pocketed it, while Monsieur tossed the crumpled candy wrapper on to the flames. Its silvery coating flared. We all sipped *kir*.

A South African exclaimed, "Dinner smells wonderful, Madame!"

A Scot agreed, then a Californian. We all agreed.

At table, Monsieur discussed the trees on the terrain we'd crossed, admiring specially the strength and longevity of the Kermes oak. In calcareous, pebbly soil it throve, indifferent to that chemistry.

We asked about the semi-deserted villages we'd walked through, the proliferating *À Louer* and *À Vendre* signs, the shut schools, ancient churchyards poorly maintained.

He considered. "Every century has its disasters. These are ours."

Madame nodded. We went on to her hazelnut cake.

All night it rained.

Next day's breakfast featured blackcurrant and apricot jams, made by *la maman et la belle-maman de Madame* from fruit grown in the hotel's garden. Croissants, homemade. We ate fresh Spanish oranges. The foresters were not at table, nor the dog in the courtyard.

Soon the tour's van arrived, to take us to the start of our climb to the site of the great burning. We looked forward to being driven. Our luggage stuffed in, we squeezed giggling on to the narrow seats as our hosts bade us farewell.

In another town at the end of that day we ate a celebratory dinner, laughing, talking, at a table crowded with
bottles and cell phones and serving dishes. As we opened
the last bottle of wine, some in our group confessed that
at dawn they'd heard barks. Opened the red shutters to
witness the dog's struggle, the men bundling her into the
funny truck.

Where to?

That query segued into *Where next?*

One must reach the airport by dawn for a Munich
flight, one for Amsterdam. Sure, share a taxi. Brilliant sig-
nage, these European airports had. A Danube cruise, old
pals in Barcelona, a family reunion in Edinburgh—happy
plans, though *It'll be good to get home* won several repeats.

Best then to wrap up the evening now, finish packing.

Bustle of bill and tip, purses closing, wallets folded.

That sheep—we spoke of her too. Her great shining
eyes, what colour? Some of us thought dark blue, some
remembered brown.

STRUGGLE

Lying awake, I become aware of the electronic machine on the back of my head. Again I suffer mind-crushing pressure. *Nora, get up!* Forced out to the kitchen, the hall, but I refuse the elevator. Trap.

Stairs dark. Down. Where do the men hide?

Dark out too. But the all-night drugstore, I'd forgotten that. Fluorescents. Relief. Shoppers' bargain bin has a plastic bike helmet, pink, the oppression of women, but it'll save my life. The strap won't untwist, my chin hurts. Still they don't see me going home, don't catch me picking up my mail.

From the Welfare. Appointment. What do they want? I won't go.

After a bowl of cornflakes I sleep well.

One Week To Go

At the campaign office with the women, seven hours today. Tired, even with the helmet. The angry men want it off. I must fight all the time.

Many in this collective are new to all political struggle, let alone to work for abortion-law repeal. They've never built a demo before, can't see the dangers. I must teach as much as work. Whoever speaks at Mother's Day will need careful coaching.

Sarah's inexperienced too, but months ago I saw her potential, gave her leaflets about our movement's weekly forums on Cuba, Quebec independence, unions, the US invasion of Grenada. She came.

Next, long talks about revolution with me, with our exec. Eleven of them. Seven men. Now she's Comrade Sarah. Could she be a cadre? So young. In branch meetings she's spoken twice. Reads, reads, takes notes.

Even with only us two assigned here, this collective's done a lot. We've got thirty endorsements for Mother's Day, not only women's groups but unions, civil liberties, teachers, students, lawyers, nurses. Church people even. All those banners waving over Cambie Bridge— bravo! Then at *our* public hospital we'll confront the right-to-lifers.

Under my chin hurts.

We all go to Woodwards' lunch counter. Sarah pays for me. Burger, chocolate shake.

When I say *Our marches must get bigger, stronger,* the women nod, nod, but don't fully realize why. The Betty Greens, Bernice Girards, respectable types in the so-called pro-life—just cover, for killers.

I listen in, eating supper at Sunset Pizza. One kingpin runs the show. He's stocky, medium height, mean-looking, drives a Suzuki jeep around my neighbourhood. His son drives another, uttering threats. If we open a clinic, they'll have the cops arrest me for the Tylenol killings. I laugh out loud, shut them up.

Like Sarah, many new comrades are students. Same, in this women's collective. Intellectuals can play a good role in the struggle but they must face facts. Canada has an organized network of extreme right-wingers, with US connections who think Reagan's too far left. They have guns. Only repeal, only mass action can keep us safe.

All afternoon at the office we arrange, decide. Who'll handle the press at the rally? Who'll sell our new buttons? Who'll speak for us? We must decide soon. Katie? She's older than many. Quiet, strong.

The phone rings. A frantic woman, turned down by the Therapeutic Abortion Committee, so-called. TAC. Attack. Three men against one woman. We give her the phone numbers. We check costs of portable toilets, proof-read the final mail-out. I can tell Sarah wishes I'd take my helmet off. I won't, can't.

On the whole, this collective has healthy politics. The women aren't sectarian. They just need help to see what can be done, to look ahead. They want a clinic. Sisters, let's examine that goal! To win, yes, many progressive elements could draw together in common action. Even doctors.

Good doctors exist, but I couldn't see the one I wanted. They said *All in your head*, shoved me into a shrink's office. He irradiated me. From his window I saw the Suzukis. Jeeps, army.

Revolutionaries ask, *Why must women struggle to create a clinic, then pay for it? Run it?* That's medicare's job. *For a free abortion clinic!* At the rally, our speaker could point the way forward with that slogan.

My helmet, that's army too. Armour.

Afterwards, Sarah and I walk to our movement's hall, talking rally. Fundraising, sound system, check. Marshals, check. The collective's speaker?

"Nora, you'd be good," Sarah says.

I would, but my head hurts. *Did I say that aloud? Say Katie?*

Under my chin, the skin's pinched. Dead tired. *Don't say that.* The hall's crowded. Someone's brought cinnamon buns. *Who told Sarah to say that to me?*

I make tea, rest in the kitchen.

The cops may declare we can't cross Cambie Bridge without a motorcycle escort. They'd ride close, blast our legs with hot exhaust. Once, at an antiwar march, a pig brushed his gauntlet against me and wiggled his tongue. The state's a body of armed men. Heading south over the bridge, we'll have northbound traffic alongside too. Scary.

If the collective obeys the cops' order, some ultra-lefts will attack us, natch. They claim Vancouver's women are ready to rise. Dangerous, foolish! Many women still trust the system. But if the collective disobeys the order, many won't march at all. Worse, they'll leave the demo. Leadership's required. The old question: What is to be done?

Our branch organizer, Annie, sends me a smile from over there in the main room, by Sarah. Two male exec members join them. Plotting? Is head-pressure starting? I touch my pink helmet, my hair. Needs washed. Working at the mill, I washed it every day, back in the day, my teens.

Another bun.

Whatever Annie's saying, Sarah's taken aback.

These basket-cases place a burden on us. I overheard that, from an earlier organizer. *Nora mustn't work alone externally. Unpredictable,* he stated, *especially under stress.* Yet for months the exec left me on my own in this collective. Our leadership doesn't grasp the radical potential of women's liberation. I never said that. I recruited Sarah.

Having crazies as members puts us at even greater disadvantage. To my face a woman leader spoke those words. *Huge forces are arrayed against us, comrade.* As if I didn't know. *Same with homos,* she added.

I've done twenty years now.

Back and forth, Sarah, Annie, Sarah. Natch, the recruit will crush her doubts, obey. Will Sarah last twenty?

My tea's cold. Scared to go home. Can't stay out all night.

At McDonalds, fries and pop. The drugstore has a new lipstick, *Bravo.* Nice bright red. No one's hiding there, or near my building, and in my apartment things seem— okay, I guess.

On the TV news, cops fill the screen. Coincidence? I turn them off. *Ha ha, serves you right!* When I'm in bed the strap hurts, though, and I remember: too many coincidences means they aren't that. A woman murdered in Coquitlam lived on what was my street, back in high school. The day I planned to attend a women's demo in Victoria, a ferry ramp collapsed, injuring three. Last week I phoned to make a doctor's appointment, hours before some MD died in a hunting "accident" near Prince George. Who'll take me as a patient now?

We could shout, *Women, don't bow to the cops! Take over the bridge, stop traffic!* That'd shut the sectarians up. Funny! But is it ultra-left?

To march, I'll need armour. Where? Where? I put my helmet on the bedside table because the strap hurts. Gone. Now I can't find the light switch. The landlord's been here, he's an agent, I knew it, he's let the men in, they've got my head, here's the machine again, crushing.

Six Days To Go

Clean hair and Bravo—that'd show Welfare I'm not disabled. My eye-bags are bad, though, bad sleep, so I stick sunglasses to my helmet. The tape's a struggle to use, takes time. I'm late to the collective.

Oh no! Three women went to the cop shop *to request* an escort. Sarah did argue that at least we shouldn't go begging. She tried. If only I'd been here to intervene, not fighting for my life at home.

Collaboration with the class enemy, some radicals will say, cowards who fear women's liberation, call it divisive. Still, a bad label.

The phones ring, ring, TAC victims, press, pro-life crazies.

We order pizza for supper. Hungry. Not enough cheese. Then it's the last mail-out, addressing envelopes to individual members, women's groups, press, radio, TV, unions, churches, donors, academics, lawyers, doctors. Write, write.

"Our postie comrades will ensure quick delivery!" Everyone laughs. Good. Rosa advised, *Be joyful in politics.*

That draws people. Yes, I'd speak well, but that wouldn't build this group.

Stuff the envelopes, seal, stamp, stuff, seal, stamp, tired.

Talk dwindles, till one says, "I had an abortion last year."

She tells. Three others tell. I don't. Sarah's pale, silent. We all cry.

At ten o'clock we walk to the main post office, shove hundreds of envelopes down the chute. Bravo! Laughing, everyone heads home.

My head hurts, chin too. Hungry. Fries and pop.

Sleepy, exhausted—but I wake at four. My helmet's off again. *Who did this?* My skin's still wrinkly from the strap. *Someone was here. I'm not stupid.* I replace my armour. Awkward, shielded head on pillow.

Was it Mr A who snuck in?

This evening while the women told, I remembered. Bad, bad.

Back in 1967, completely illegal, before even the TACs.

If I'd phoned my Mum—first, hysterics.

Jesus then, on and on.

Then she'd have called out to Dad, at the TV. He was big, still strong even with his bad arm from the chainsaw, still had his driver's license. They both hated our movement. In minutes he'd head up the ramp to the freeway. Where could I hide in this city?

If I had it, how to tell them? She'd die of shame. He'd kill me.

And if I'd talked to Jim, before I was certain?

You screwed someone else. I knew it.

No, no, we just had a drink!

Nora, you're not putting this on me. You take care of it.
Jim said all of that anyway, after the test.
Said, *You have to have it. You're too far along.*
I said, *I can't. They'll kill me. I'm not.*
Now there's Sarah. Her clothes, how she talks—
she's had it easy in life. She can't know the dangers.
The traps.

Five Days To Go

At our office, a few regulars don't show. I reassure
the women—it's common, in the run-up to a big action.
"We're still here!"

They laugh. We answer the phone, head out to do pos-
tering, pick up leaflets from the printer, buy trash bags.
Back at the office, test the rented loud-hailer, laugh. We
review expenses. With a good collection, we'll break even.

Desperate women call.

Sarah's quiet. Words press inside her. What has she
been told to tell me?

Heaviness at the hall for the weekly forum, after the
day's work. Heavy. My pink helmet pinches. It's hard to
understand the comrade speaking on the Irish struggle.
Handsome. Won't notice me, natch.

In question period, the chair ignores Sarah's raised
hand. Public rejection—so the exec knows. *You haven't
spoken to Nora yet.* Yet. She blushes. I could tell her it's a
test. She's being rated.

After beer and chips, I head home. Three drunk young
women on the bus get loud. I'm polite, but they shout
Fatty fatty two by four! They grab my head, pull my helmet

off and leave the bus, laughing and waving. I have to ride on unprotected.

Why should I tell Sarah anything? She'll learn or she won't.

Exposed.

At home I can't be like that, so I walk to a park and sit on a bench with my hands on my head, but my arms soon hurt, and weirdos sleep there. At my building, I go on hands and knees behind the dumpster. Cold metal feels solid. I'll survive. I even doze.

When the garbage roars at dawn, I struggle out. The driver gawks, and I laugh. The stairs feel clear, the hall-way too. My place doesn't echo badly. Bruises, scratches on my neck. Jeans torn.

After cornflakes I sleep in my chair. No crusher comes.

Four Days To Go

Mr A's in my head the instant I wake up.

First I tried a sympathetic doctor who'd given money to the repeal campaign. An older woman comrade then suggested a nurse who didn't *do* abortions but sometimes assisted. Jim found Mister A at last. A for Awful.

I ran a fever, after. Everything hurt. That nurse came then. Left some pills.

"Has to be goddamn ninety-eight point six," she kept saying. "Ninety-eight point six. Jesus Christ, mister, you hear me?"

I heard her. I didn't hear Jim. I couldn't speak. I'm not religious. The radio went on about Confederation and Expo.

"By supper-time, or get her to goddamn Emergency!"

Jim shoved the thermometer into me, shoved. We didn't go. Recovery took forever. I couldn't get out at all. We broke up. I knew we would but he spoke first. I hadn't the strength.

Missing so many shifts, I lost my waitress job. No union, natch. Way back at the mill there was, but our strike got crushed. I asked Jim for rent money to get started. I'd pay him back.

Okay. He gave me cash.

Such a nice morning! I went out, the first time in weeks, and bussed downtown to look at rooms. Picked a nice one, right near the hall, but when I got back he'd gone. Taken all his stuff. I couldn't find him. No one would tell. Some comrades knew. I know that.

Nights, I heard Jim through the wall, *Ha ha, fatty!* He'd only quit if I got up to eat, watch TV. The fat-coat felt safe. For a while. *Stop thinking that. Stop.*

Daytimes, talking out loud can help.

Nora, go to work with the women. They look at me funny. *No they don't. They respect you.* Welfare wants rid of me. *Stop.* They want to Disable me, put me inside. *Stop this!* I get off the bus early, by Zellers, and they've got the exact same helmet, just purple. Right away, relief, but the cashier gives me a dirty look. Dirty. She tickles my palm, giving change, and the heaviness comes on.

So many women at the office! Sarah's got them to sort out who'll protect the rally site during the march. They've confirmed the toilets, too. Good work. We all smile. Sarah's the age I was with Dr A.

Who'll decide when the march starts? Me. A moment comes: the crowd's thick enough, or a certain quiet thinness means it won't grow any more.

Route details next. Lane change at the bridge ramp. Offer leaflets to sidewalk-watchers, invite them in. Only trust marshals with sparkly armbands. Who heads the first-aid crew? Music at front middle back of march, never silent all through, never. Chants. Song sheets. Hecklers, cops.

If you're provoked, the pricks win. *Did I say that aloud?*

This purple armour doesn't cover as the pink did. I'm exposed. Not just Sarah's looking at me. *Stop.* On through the list. Women with kids walk in the middle. Safer. Who'll have walkie-talkies? We'll shout our slogans. If the demo's big, other slogans may be "off."

"Don't argue, just shout louder!" That gets a laugh.

Sarah answers the phone, gives the numbers. Her face says the woman's crying hard. Onward. The rally. Guarding the chair, the kids' area, collection buckets, mics, speakers. Who's allowed on stage? *No one else.* Who'll do clean-up? Count people? Count money?

All morning. Hungry. Hard to walk, heavy as lead. Nearly dead. *Did I say that? Don't.* The dream where you can't move. Can't struggle.

I find strength to get up. In the washroom I wet some paper towels, wipe my face. Sweaty under my purple armour, yet cold, trembly. Something's big in me. Here's Sarah. Where'd she hide?

"I can take you home, Nora. You're not feeling well, are you?"

Predictable.

"We'll get a cab, ok?"

You don't fool me, missy. Drivers have taken me there before.

"Just to the hall, rest a bit?"

Annie's there. The exec's there. Sarah will exhibit me. I showed her, led her, took her seriously. *Only for a women's group,* leading men said about me. Leading women didn't disagree.

Stop this, Nora!

And I do.

"I'm just tired, Sarah. Hungry." I dry my face.

Getting mad's made me feel better. I can walk now. We go back together to the office, where I smile. "Time for lunch!" We haven't settled on our own speaker, leave that for after, but I know what needs to be said. I'll coach Katie.

Off to Woodwards we go, and on the way I see the men trying to hide behind that dumb steam clock. *Ha ha!* The time's wrong, my helmet's full of my head, no space no air, they can't get in.

Sarah sits by me. Boss, jailer?

My choice is lemon pie. Miss Clever's too.

I start before she can. "Who do you think should speak?"

Sarah blinks. "You don't want to?"

Sweet meringue, dissolving.

"Good leaders encourage others to lead, to gain experience."

"Annie said to stop you."

Sour yellow. Our organizer's accused me of forgetting the basics of movement-building, after two decades.

Heavy again. Can I move, let alone run? This lemon's poison.

"The collective needs to grow, Sarah, to make its own mistakes. That way, women will learn to fight better. Understand more. Maybe become open to revolutionary ideas, too."

Beyond heavy. Stuck. Thick.

"Choose Katie!"

The floor rises, tilts, heaves me sideways. *Funny fatty, you broke the chair! E*verything tilts back, rightwards, no right-winger, never, but here come the men with the crusher to finish me off.

Three Days To Go

Two Days To Go

Tomorrow

Mother's Day

Some Other Other Day

Two of the psych ward's windows overlook a bus stop. I stand so I can't be seen from the street, peek out—and a Suzuki jeep zips round the corner. So obvious. It won't return till next time I look. Now regular cars go by, red grey grey blue, red grey grey blue, but as soon as I see that trick they throw in a black, a beige. They can't fool me.

Fur-mouth. Dry mouth. Staff stole my Bravo. I'm dead pale.

A bus arrives. Eleven people get off. Ordinary-looking. Clever. Seven men, same as on the branch exec. Sarah gets off last. She's not on the exec. Yet. She looks up. I jump back, bump into that angry woman who won't wash. She wants staff to hold her down and pull her clothes off. There's a male aide she likes. He's after me all the time. I defend myself.

Who told Sarah I'm here? I know nothing about Mother's Day. Who spoke? No newspapers here. Staff block TV news. I didn't march.

The sidewalk's empty, so the pro-lifers are inside the huge hospital. They'll hide wherever, and anyway they're dressed like doctors, visitors. Normal, free to be. I worked so hard, I couldn't march, but I know those faces. If they get in here I'll denounce them.

I'm not disabled. I'll get out. I have, before.

Sarah's through the lobby. In the elevator, rising. Those blue and orange arrows on the hallway floor—I haven't cracked the code. She has, but the locked double doors stop her cold. Staff speak at her through that black thing on the wall. They think I don't hear, can't understand.

No, no visitors yet.

I couldn't say.

Call ahead.

Call a head.

A head.

CALM

Strong feet stepped into the boy's dream, came nearer down the hall, and he sat up, but the sounds went past, outside.

Quick, to the window.

Down the dark quiet street came four horses, two by two, with police on top. Streetlights shone on the animals' rumps, the riders' yellow vests. Clop clop. Harnesses glinted, tails waved, manes lifted and subsided. The horses too wore reflective yellow, in bands round their ankles. No heavy traffic here, though, not like the last time he'd seen them, at rush hour, walking calmly single file between a moving bus and a line of parked cars.

Hesitation. *Bad.* His bruises still hurt.

I have to know where you are, she'd said, you can't just wander alone. You don't know this big city. And stay out of the Park! Who knows what's hiding there?

Also, they'd taken his keys.

Clothes—he found them.

As he felt in the "secret" pocket of her rain jacket, from the other bedroom came sounds he disliked. Good, they'd sleep soon.

He left the building via the rusty fire escape off the third-floor hall. At the bottom he must swallow, then jump down to damp earth—better than taking the dim stairs to the basement door.

He hurried then. Clop clop, and the horses headed west past shabby low-rises like his, past the corner store with posters stuck on its outer wall. One said *Resist!* What? Then past the school, the one he went to, with a map of all Canada on the classroom wall. Vancouver, a dot. The town where he'd lived before, not even that. On the bewildering drive to the city, she'd kept saying *Look at the map, see where you're going!* He didn't. Hadn't ever asked to make this move. Back there, the cops only had motorcycles.

The boy kept half a block between himself and clop-clop, scuttling from hedge to street-tree to shrub. Where did they live? He'd seen them often, on busy West End streets or near the big beach. Sometimes the police halted them, so people could ask questions or even pat those enormous heads. He saw the cops' holsters close up, and the animals' big nostrils, and their strange eyes, bluish-brown. Such big teeth. Soon the horses moved on. Their steady gait—lots of videos showed that, how the animals just kept on coming, calm amidst furious crowds. Did riots happen here?

As the quartet neared the big street he stayed further back, waiting while the traffic light changed and changed again. On the restaurant at the corner, someone had half-scraped off a *Resist!* poster. Near this intersection, he did know his way. Homeless men slept in store entrances, their hidden faces probably familiar to him from the network of local alleys, of bins behind cafes and groceries. Once he'd taken home a cold burger, untouched in its box. They'd found it. *Bad.*

When green shone a third time he sauntered across, then hastened after the lifting hooves. Along these blocks, richer landscaping fronted tall condos. To hide and move and hide: easy. Ahead waited greater darkness, though moonlight came and went as the clouds moved.

By day he'd wandered this terrain south of Lost Lagoon, grasping at its geography. Some lamp posts in the Park and at its edges displayed a map, for tourists, so he'd learned some main routes. In the middle of the map's big green stood a tiny, surprising coyote. He hadn't known they could live in cities. Mum said *You never see what's right under your nose.* Not true. On his own he'd spotted a real raccoon snoozing in a tree, and a dead bird with a beak like a sword, and sleeping bags inside bushes, along with piled bottles and cans.

Once he'd even circled the Lagoon, peering up at the forest north of it, but had never entered the Park after sunset. In the small town, he with other kids spent hours nightly in the local park, only vacating when the teenagers took over, but no map was needed. You could see right across.

Now he followed the horses into the dark. Near-silence, but for the stepping animals. One lifted its tail. Plop plop, and that warm smell mixed with the night's leafy earthiness.

Would they turn at the tennis courts, head for the Bay? No. A right turn. Where to? At first following the horses, the boy then dared to move sideways into the damp understory of salal, laurel, giant rhodo—and then ahead, to crouch and peek as the nodding heads approached. Even when a rare midnight car drove past, the animals didn't change pace. The videos showed that too, horses proceeding while police trainers waved flags and noisemakers in their faces, fired blanks, came unseen from behind to beat garbage-can lids. Calm.

Next they went west. On one side of that road, he knew, lay open lawn, on the other just patchy shrubs, low. All the way, streetlights. Now what? Could he scrabble downhill, unseen, unheard, to the underpass, and so move roughly west too? His insides heaved. No, not that tunnel in the dark—nor by day. It curved, so the exit wasn't visible from the entrance. *I'm not a little boy any more. I'm not!* They'd laughed till they cried, though later Mum said *Sorry,* and then they smoked. Also, the meadow beyond the underpass gave no cover.

He slowed, guessing, and turned from the horses, south and then west in a long watchful arc through both open and wooded areas. Breathed leaves, a trace of skunk, of cigarette. Uphill then, on to the high bank overlooking the ocean. Here he squatted under a shore-pine distorted by wind and weather, smelled algae, watched the incoming tide's long frills of white collapse on the sand. Soaked runners, cold sockless feet—he didn't care, looked north. *I was right.* Only a hundred metres away the quartet walked towards a ramp that sloped to the beach. Touching the concrete, the lead animals snorted, and the riders spoke gently, stroking.

When hooves met beach the four horses trotted south almost as far as the point, almost gone from view—then back again, under the boy's high perch, to and fro, to and fro. The animals' muscles created light patterns on their coats while the waves gleamed under the moon, fell into silver-marbled froth and made their *hssshing* sound.

When the riders headed straight at the water, the boy gasped. He couldn't swim. Nodding, the horses waded in. They stepped freely, splashed, came back to shore, reversed and went forward again into the waves, whinnying. *They're happy!* The riders turned them tightly, splashing through the shallows as if in an enclosure rather than the Pacific. Turn, turn—and out of the water they came, dripping, tossing their manes, to shoulder sideways, back and forth, steady pairs dancing while the sand bounced up by their hooves.

They stopped. One cop said something, and within a minute the horses walked two by two up the ramp and trotted eastward into treed darkness. Where?

Clop clop, clop clop, fading. At last the boy felt cold.

Once he slipped on wet leaves, falling.

Without the horses ahead, he got muddled in the darkness.

Emerging from the Park, he found the street wasn't his but took it anyway, for traffic lights winked ahead. *Resist!* was stapled to four street trees.

At the corner he checked a tourist map. *I'm just two blocks over.* By day he'd go again, figure out the lay of the land. As the signal changed, he noted at the map's edge a legend matching images to numbers dotted on the Park's green expanse. Seven: tiny horse. *Police Stables.*

Somehow the key's noise woke them at home. *Bad.* His wet, dirty clothes enraged his mother. The man never needed a reason, but used that one too.

In bed at last, he thought a bit about how one day he'd shove them off, shove as if they were an enormous ball, six feet in diameter, rolling about a training ring to impede his progress. As horses do when skilled in crowd control, he'd shoulder them. Lean against them, step sideways, step and step and another patient step till, like him now, they'd have no choice. Steady he'd be, calm.

Mostly he imagined stables. He'd stand close, look up. Touch? Feed? Once he'd seen a girl hold out an apple. Big teeth showed as the hairy lips lifted back, and the horse crunched the fruit.

The boy raised his hand, held his palm flat.

WING NUT

I

During lunch hour, a man reached over the school fence and picked up a child registered in Senior Kindergarten. A Grade Three girl saw. Screaming, she rushed across the playground to grab an adult arm. Pursuit. Though the abductor had a good start, the teachers were younger. He dropped the boy, ran hard, escaped into the neighbourhood's leafy alleys, and remained at large when school ended.

Ignorant Moira arrived at Queen Charlotte Elementary to collect her son. Hours earlier she'd turned off her phone to concentrate, i.e., stare at a screen where each new phrase read worse than its predecessor. *I've always wanted real time for this. Why can't I do it?* She flung out of the house early, to walk the yellow-gold streets of autumn and calm herself. *I've got till New Year's. Lots of time.*

Moira hoped to see Peter first, to guess the quality of his day at this new school, *1908* incised in granite on its front. The dignified building pleased her, as did the houses nearby, weathered brick with narrow-paned windows. Tall trees stood guardian round the block.

Already kids fought leaf-wars by the steps. *I'm late again.* Peter stood alone, serious, dropping bright leaves.

"Guess what, Mum!" He jumped about. "A toilet spilled over and water went all down the big stairs!"

Moira smiled at his teacher. No return smile.

"But we didn't see any poo. Why? How does a plunger work?"

The teacher muttered, "We'll be in touch," turned to another parent.

What's that about?

"To Emerald Park, Peter?"

"No, the twisty way home," and he ran ahead.

The local alleys, some still plain dirt, angled past more than a few giant Douglas firs and Western red cedars, relics of Vancouver's ancient forest. Some wooden garages had once been stables, even settlers' cottages. *Such wide boards.* Where concrete pads supported recycling bins, outhouses once stood. *Before that, what? Who?*

Kicking leaves, Peter talked overflow all the way home—post-war stucco, small, a rental prison till Ted's insurance company promoted him or Moira wrote a bestseller—and through Pick-Up Sticks, dinosaurs, Lego.

Ted made a new audience during dinner.

"For real? Down the stairs?" Eyebrows up.

"Dad, I'll show you where!"

"Didn't anything else happen today in SK?"

"The janitor's plunger is way bigger than ours, Dad."

Before bath time father and son tried out the household's device, laugh, splash. Moira frowned out the kitchen window at the spindly new street trees.

Now, my novel. Dreaded novel. Dreadful novel?

First, her phone. Three texts from Susan, all *Must talk!* or similar.

Sighing, Moira tapped. The women, neighbours and new in the city, had met while registering their sons in school.

"Oh this kidnapping, awful!"

"This *what*?" Listening, Moira frowned. "Peter just talked about a toilet."

"Well, he's younger."

Moira sighed. Susan liked noting that Liam's birthday was *ages ago*.

"What about the——the taken kid?"

"In the *other* SK. The principal's email says he's fine. She'll report at the meeting this week."

You believe her? But the boys played well enough together, so the call continued. Afterwards, she didn't even open her novel but discussed the whole thing with Ted.

For days, all the parents discussed the whole thing. How to detect their offspring's trauma (if any)? *Stranger danger,* just a nostrum? Didn't this man simply scoop up a kid? Why wouldn't more parents offer to supervise? Couldn't someone make a schedule? The school's website said little about safety: shocking.

"Cops?" asked Ted, as he headed out of town for another false car insurance claim. "Security cameras? A higher fence? Hello?"

Like cottonwood pollen, word floated about. The father of Tyler, the abducted child, would attend the meeting. No, he wouldn't.

The mother? "Not in the picture."

Meaning what? Why didn't Tyler cry out?

In the school gym, Moira and Susan sat with far more parents than usual.

"My report." Ms Almstedt reviewed facts, actions, new protocols. Then, to repress the swelling parental verbiage so eager for release, the principal stated, "Better for the kids, for us all, not to *dwell* on this unfortunate incident. Questions only, please."

Susan nodded hard. Moira's brows rose.

Idiot. But how can I make <u>real</u> friends, stuck all day at my desk?

Next, Ms Almstedt asked the attending policewoman to report.

"The investigation's active and ongoing."

"Thank you, officer. Now, on to planning Parents' Night. Please meet with your child's teacher."

I've always longed for time. Even when Peter was tiny, I tried. Yes, for hours Moira did "write," walking the colicky screamer. Few drafts or even notes resulted. *Before that, work.* Writing tech manuals all day, crushing her creativity.

Baulked, Moira moved with Susan to the SK parental group.

The teacher smiled. "We'll have an art gallery!"

Each tree on the school's block had been assigned to several students. In good weather, kids would go out to draw "their" trees. They'd pick a seedpod or nut, and wax a leaf, to display by their drawings.

"Plus it's a social."

Susan volunteered cookies. Moira, squares. Heading home, she mockingly enacted parents competing for prominence for "My kid's tree!"

Susan didn't crack a smile.

II

Before pick-up, the two mums walked round the school's block.

Moira could identify few of the guardian trees. Mostly old. Big. Some had heaved the sidewalks into asphalt-patched waves, others had long ago intertwined their branches and now bore the scars of city chainsaws. One tree resembled a head of stringy leafy hair, just clearing the ground. Another's roots arched and stretched in a dark rigid web above the grass, clear to the next lamp-post.

"Dangerous!" Susan.

Under this broad bulky tree lay a scatter of brown seeds, frilled, light as moths on Moira's hand.

On their release, the boys wanted to show off "their" trees.

"Mine first!" Peter ran ahead.

Liam stalled. "No fair!"

Susan said, "You're the big boy, remember?"

"Here's *my* Camperdown elm."

"Oh Peter, lucky you!" Moira laughed.

"Go in, Mum."

He held back the strings, let them fall again into a supple leathery curtain. Shielded, the women crouched inside with their giggling boys.

"*I* saw this tree first," said Liam, "but *I*—"

"We always came here when—"

"Don't butt in! Mum, come see my tree *now*."

Mothers followed sons.

Susan frowned. "Weird in there."

"Lovely! Almost invisible."

Liam shouted, "*My* tree has bright leaves!"

Tall, slim, the Bowhall maple speared red-gold against blue sky.

"But we can't go *into* yours."

"But mine's called *flame* tree, and *arrow* tree. Your name's dumb."

The boys then claimed ignorance of all other trees on the block and pressed for Dairy Queen, Pick-Up Sticks, battling dinosaurs, Lego.

That evening Moira visited the city's website.

Prior to World War I, local homeowners had preempted the Park Board's scheme for uniform street trees around the new school. Led by a university botanist and the head gardener at the new lunatic asylum, Riverview, they'd acquired unusual saplings—gingko, catalpa, tulip tree, wing nut. Post-Versailles, officialdom reached Queen Charlotte, but the city arborist refused to uproot the flourishing trees. A tradition developed. If a tree died, the same species replaced it. One photo on the site showed the seeds of the bulky wing nut, still the city's only specimen on public land.

Still. Moira smiled at the delicate shapes.
Noticed the hour.
Covered her eyes. *I haven't written a word.*
Inadequate sleep followed.

III

News: an arrest.

The police charged a male, 42, with no fixed address but a long record of exposure, petty theft, attempted abduction. Since his teens he'd done time in correctional facilities and those for the mentally ill.

For these facts, Ms Almstedt suggested age-appropriate wordings. She urged, *Don't let youngsters watch local news. Don't leave newspapers lying about.*

On the adult word-winds, *crazy deviant pedophile* dispersed.

Also, *Such a relief!*

Another feeling rose too, harder to name. The *Herald* photo showed a Caucasian man, medium height, nondescript features, thinning hair, a mid-section probably thicker than in youth. In a line-up with the SK dads only his clothes would stand out, his dirty green jacket too ragged to be cool.

"Do we wish he *looked* bad?" Moira asked Susan, waiting at school. "What does that even *mean?*" Silence.

In Emerald Park, with other mums they debated cursive writing while children jumped in huge leaf piles, till Liam fell and cried.

At the cafe, Susan used Ms Almstedt's lingo. "That bad man's been caught." The boys ate choc-chip muffins. Moira drank espresso, didn't verbalize thoughts about *bad,* considered reaching the reporter who'd filed the story.

That night she learned that a tree's roots extend at least as wide as its branches, sometimes even as long as thrice the tree's height. This root-web, in cities hidden under concrete, asphalt, mown boulevards, continually grows.

Gingko, a living fossil.

Tulip tree, named for its leaf shape.

Today's urban planners choose the Bowhall maple for parking lots because of its slender habit. *How depressing.*

And Camperdown? On an estate so named in Scotland a long-ago gardener noticed a *mutant contorted wych elm.* He grafted a spur on to a normal wych. *Why?* Every Camperdown's lineage, Peter's included, traced back to that mutant. *Wych elm. Witch tree? Is wych witch?* In the annoying way of English, yes no maybe. *Wych.* Germanic base. *Weak.* "Term applied to various plants and trees having pliant limbs."

At the *Herald*'s website, Moira identified the reporter, Constance.

Getting ready for bed, she pictured the elm's witchy hair. Half-recalled a university lecture about a mythic being in a tree. Greek? Old English? And heard absent Ted. *You've got all day to write. Why can't you get it done?* He'd agreed to her six-month break from library school, for writing, though it lengthened their days in stucco prison.

"Mum?"

A smaller voice.

"Honey, what's wrong? Bad dream?"

Moira hummed lullabies till Peter slept again, loving his hair-veiled nape. His eyelashes, concealing. His limbs, the skin flawless but for scabs pleasurably picked off and shots inflicted to keep him safe.

Because it doesn't interest me. Again she lay awake.

IV

Update:

The fleeing molester climbed a large cedar and sat for hours amid thick green lace, invisible on high. A police dog barked, barked but got yanked away by her choke-chain. At dusk the man climbed down. Slept somewhere that night, elsewhere another. In a dodgy 7-Eleven he'd just pocketed two KitKats when the clerk pressed her emergency call button.

From his bedroom, Peter shouted, "Mum, come!" Scrunched-up drawings of the Camperdown lay about. "I can't make it *go* right." Eyes shining, angry.

After a cuddle and a snack, a video.

Close by her child as dinosaurs lurched about primordial swamps, bashing trees with their tails and trying to murder each other, Moira glanced over her morning's work. *I can't either. Who'm I kidding?*

"I wish Ted were home," she told Susan, at once regretting the confidence.

"Don't you like being alone? For your writing?" Susan's voice insinuated the art's kinship with other disorders spoken of as *my*—rosacea, bursitis.

"Something's upset Peter. His father sees things I don't."

Tactless, to a single parent. True though. So, too bad. Moira ended the call, and planned a special dinner for next day.

Ted, arriving home, grinned. "Smells good!"

He sat comfortably flipping through the *Herald*, while Moira set the table and Peter built a Lego prison for hostages taken in dinosaur wars.

"Look, son, some guy out on the street in a pumpkin costume, weeks before Halloween. Wing nut!"

Wide eyes looked. Registered disappointment. "Who's *he*?"

"Some crazy guy. How's your dino going to escape?"

Peter started a bridge. "But we called our *friend* Wing Nut."

"Who?"

"The man who came to play with us at school."

The parents stilled.

"Inside the elm tree."

Ted moved to the floor, to help build. "What did you play?"

A shrug. "He told us stories. And we got a wing nut, every time."

Dino jumped over the bridge towards his green companions. Heroic feet dotted the silence.

"Wing Nut said he might have to go away soon."

"Why?" Moira asked.

"Might not say goodbye, even." A tremor, there.

The oven timer sounded. Unattended, it would go on, on.

"But we'd have the tree." Peter's face contorted. "To remember."

"The elm?" Ted asked, as Moira returned from the kitchen.

"*No*, Daddy! His *own* tree, the Wing Nut."

Dead moths. Rigid roots, stretching as far as the eye couldn't see.

"Could you show me?"

Peter hit his tower. Lego tumbled. "No! Daddy, you never came to see where the toilet water went!"

"Son—how about Pick-Up Sticks instead?"

"No! *Boring*."

Moira served, wondering when that once-loved game had died.

While Ted did bedtime (laughter sounded), she went online.

Where was the abductor held? On what charge? Could she attend the trial? How to find out? *I don't know.* Any local jails? Yes, plus photos. Surprise. Near a trailhead out of Emerald Park stood an edifice of Tyndall stone, seen a hundred times: The Stoddard. Minimum security.

Susan would have a fit.

At the *Herald*'s site, Moira located Constance. Typed. Sent.

Ted's footsteps, another surprise.

"Aren't you writing?"

"Research." *Another writing hour, gone.*

He stood over her. "You can't believe Peter's story."

"Why would he lie?"

"Daily, outside the school fence? Preposterous, just like the toilet. All day I deal with liars, Moira. That's my job."

"But that man did hide up a tree. Something *real* happened."

"Yes, Peter *really* wants attention."

"You don't know for sure."

Ted sighed. "I know you pretend things. Like your writing."

"I what?"

The fight veered into irrelevance, for Moira failed to see the crucial role of wing nuts in carpentry and cabinetry. Proving his point, Ted turned her favourite armchair upside down to rip off the fabric covering the springs.

"Those are *real*."

Moira stamped, slammed into their bedroom.

He slept on the sofa.

V

Drawn elm trees appeared in the recycling, also on the floor of Peter's room. Pick-Up Sticks rolled about too. *Their box?* Crayons, toffee wrappers. *Where'd he get those?* No picture showed anyone in the Camperdown. Still, she phoned Susan.

"Peter said *what?*"

"Could be nothing, just wondered if Liam...?"

"Your. Son. Tells. Stories."

"The man *said* he might have to go away without warning. Susan, he gave the boys *presents*."

"Lies." Click.

Online, Moira found female and male bolts, screws, wings, wing nuts, wing-nuts, wingnuts. American wing-nuts were Tea Party-ers. Nuts nut-bars crazy batty. To attract pollinators, Wing Nuts in spring bore long spikes of yellow flowers.

Constance emailed. *Stoddard, likely. A year at least.*

VI

When Moira found the school principal unavailable, she made an appointment. She and Peter then walked down Queen Charlotte's leaf-strewn steps right next to Susan and Liam. Silence.

Do I call Hello?

Peter began gabbling, a boy at the art table, a big mess. Moira smiled. "Was his name Peter?"

"No, Mum!" Affronted, "You don't know everything."

They went to Emerald Park, had fun.

Before the next Parents' Night planning session, Ted offered to go.

"So you can write."

Moira accepted this peace token, and in the quiet opened her novel.

Read twenty-three pages. Tedious pages. Weak, thin. *It's all just me, called She or Her.*

Closing the file, she went online to research the supervision of school playgrounds. Angry, foul-mouthed parents, some unable to spell or punctuate, vilified teachers for chatting about date nights and plotting union politics while kids fell or got pushed off swings. Unnoticed, children humiliated their classmates, fought, went out of bounds to meet teen dealers.

Ted started the moment he got home.

"You told Susan about Peter's nonsense?"

"She had to know!"

"Susan's raising her boy alone. Tough. Why trouble her?"

"How about Tyler's father? He's a single parent too."

"Your point?"

"That the story could be *true*."

Ted jammed his coat onto its hook. "Anyway. We got it all planned. How to display the kids' drawings, the leaves and all."

"Bully for you and Susan."

His turn for the bedroom.

Moira stayed online.

A century before, one name proposed for Vancouver's new loony bin, funny farm, bughouse was *Hospital of the Mind*.

A bio of that long-ago city arborist noted that his daughter lived seventy years as a patient in Riverview. By the time she died, the specimen trees he'd planted on the lawns sloping towards the Fraser had all attained full height.

Twentieth-century science proved that gardens helped to calm, to heal. Today's architects all include green spaces when designing hospitals. Germany, Scandinavia—marvellous examples.

Enough!

In the hallway Moira hesitated. Joined her husband in their bed.

VII

Heading for the school, she noted several cedars capable of sheltering a climber. Such trees, like glacial erratics abandoned by the frozen flow, kept the past present. How old? In Vancouver's general clear-cut, who'd decided not to fell them? Had local cedars been transformed into canoes, long ago? How long?

In the school playground, a bike shed and a jungle gym interrupted sight lines, and hedges veiled parts of the chain-link. Watchers would need to move constantly.

Walking home, Moira said, "Peter, that man, your friend in the elm tree?"

He stopped. "I don't want to talk about him."

"I like hearing about your friends. Keep going!"

"Can I get a doughnut?"

"You had cookies in your lunch."

He clung, manufacturing sobs. "I can't walk so far. Carry me, Mum!"

"You're a big boy, Peter." She sat down on the sidewalk, a tactic devised when he was three. "I'll wait." The tantrum lasted seven minutes.

At the health-food store, Moira bought two iced Halloween doughnuts. Mother and son ate them at home while paging through a dinosaur book.

"He told us not to."

Her mouth all sugar, she couldn't think what Peter meant.

"So I won't talk about him. Ever." He turned a page, his roots invisible.

VIII

Having rehearsed, Moira spoke fluently.

Mrs Almstedt frowned. "He inveigled kindergarten boys over the fence and no one noticed?"

"They hid *in* the elm. Playground visibility's poor. I've checked."

Frown.

"He just *lifted* the child, remember? Tyler didn't struggle or call for help."

"That was a field trip day. Many teachers absent. The subs evidently weren't familiar with our procedures." Smile.

"They weren't informed?"

No smile. "We've made changes—but Peter's tale remains [*will she say preposterous? fantastic?*] incredible."

"You won't discuss my concerns with your staff?"

"The offender's been sentenced." A faint smile.

"Yes, to Stoddard."

I have information too, Mrs A.

IX

At Parents' Night, Peter's hairy elm and the thirteen laboured letters circling it looked no cruder than many drawings on display. The yellow double-serrate leaf, waxed, showed well on green paper alongside the useless seed.

He smiled up at his work. Then, "Dad, the toilet, come see!"

Alone, Moira moved along the display, viewing a red-crayon Scotch pine, a blue Norway maple, copper beech leaves, drupes of purple-leaf plum—and now Liam's neat, bright Bowhall, complete with artist and mother.

"Good!" Moira gestured. "Hello!"

Nothing.

From across the room, she heard *Tyler* and saw an ordinary man, arm around an ordinary boy, talking with other parents.

Tyler's rough strokes did show the wing nut's shape. The roots thrust up, up. *I can't write even that well.* Under his tree stood a woman, smiling. *In his picture!* Tears, nearly. Frilled nuts, too fragile to tape, hung in a Ziplock.

In the wych elm, did Tyler get presents? Did he scramble laughing into Wing Nut's arms, to the other boys' envy?

"Mum!" Peter pulled at her. "I showed Dad!"

They'd met the janitor, seen the plunger.

"In-dus-tri-al size." Giggling, Peter ran to his classmates.

"Tree roots completely blocked the plumbing." Ted smiled. "Our boy didn't exaggerate much."

"So—what about his elm quote *story?*"

"I did ask Peter."

"You mean you accused him of lying!"

"I *asked*, Moira. He's not telling."

Then the staff welcomed parents to the low SK tables, for treats.

The two boys and Ted gobbled, giggled, while Susan and Moira ignored each other's baking.

"Good night," they managed.

X

Halloween.

Peter and Liam begged to trick or treat together. "Pleeeeease, mum!"

The guardian mothers accommodated, while enrolling their boys in different winter sports and fostering new friendships for them.

At Christmas, a man entered Susan's picture.

Moira trashed her novel on New Year's Day.

Back in library school she studied hard, learning multiple ways to find out.

Yellow strings waved on the wing nut, the elm's green curtain formed, the Bowhall sharpened its bright arrowhead. When tiny green velociraptors *zzzz*-ed in the back yard, Ted set up a hummingbird-feeder, and overnight Peter quit dinosaurs for their descendants. What local trees did which birds like for nests? Did some pairs return to the same one? He began a spotting notebook.

"A real hobby!" Moira and Ted gave him junior binoculars.

In Emerald Park, Peter himself spotted a bushtit nest under construction. Formed of spiderweb, moss, and grasses, it hung, sock-like, on a vine-maple branch, shielded by new leaves. He visited daily. At the library he found videos, magazines. His parents smiled.

Then that one branch died. The leaves, shrivelling, exposed the nest. The birds abandoned the building site.

Peter sobbed for a week. "They lost their special house! For why?"

XI

With Moira's library-science degree in hand, the couple decided she might as well go for a master's while she was at it.

Promoted, Ted travelled less. Now his workshops trained others to assess car-insurance claimants—injured, often grief-stricken, and lying through their teeth.

In the second lovely spring, Moira met Constance at a party.

"Who? Oh, him. Halfway house now, I think."

Moira didn't dwell on this, or consider the term's oddity, because she was there with people who were steadily growing into real friends.

She didn't tell Susan of course.

Nor Ted, though that decision took a while.

Moira's thesis filled her. Sometimes, rarely, she pictured the man at liberty, perhaps even nearby, but neither heard nor read of what had happened. She job-hunted, and then focussed on her satisfying work as a reference librarian.

As the trees transformed a third time, Ted and Moira and Peter bought their own brick house, near the school and as old. Incarceration ended! Along their new street bloomed tall horse chestnuts, white pink red, all in a row with gone-tooth gaps where the rot had won. Roots heaved up the boulevard.

"They go right under our house!" Peter laughed.

Moira, packing happily, wondered *How'd we accumulate so much stuff?*

Even their boy had. Shelves once packed with nursery rhymes and fairy tales now held a dried-out honeycomb, pinned butterflies and spiders, eggshells, a hummingbird nest with two tiny feathers, a corn snake's skin. His old story books waited, stacked, in the closet. Behind them, Pick-Up Sticks. So beloved! Moira, smiling, tipped the cardboard cylinder over. Only a dozen wing nuts tumbled out, brown, dusty, flaking and fragmenting as broken moths do.

APOLOGY

"Edith," those four women said, "you've been inconsiderate."

Thoughtless, they continued. Unsympathetic. Less than kind. Etc.

An intervention, no less. Over coffee and cookies, prepared by me, in my apartment.

First on their list: Jocelyn. Rather, *poor Jocelyn*.

The story?

At the victory party for our provincial candidate, who'd lost, I bought a raffle ticket. Number 63, then my age. First prize: from a local "fine foods" shop, a heaping basket of nuts, biscuits, chocolates, cheeses, jars of olives, etc., all wrapped in crisp starry gold paper and doubtless stale.

Our group, Jocelyn included, awaited the draw. During the campaign she and I had done phone canvassing together, side-by-side in a booth with the awkward scripts before us. Often she'd deviate. "Oh, you're cooking supper? I'll call back!" Wasted time drags down the work. She never finished her lists.

Jocelyn's ticket was Number 64.

"Such fun to win! Sixty-five next birthday." That wistful girlish smile. "I'd throw a little party, and share the basket!"

Smiles, pats for Jocelyn, and the draw was called.

The quote festive season was then upon us, so on Boxing Day I set the gift basket in the lobby of my apartment building. It emptied soon.

Jocelyn and I met again at a New Year's Day open house.

"Oh Edith, are you enjoying your basket? Such a good selection, I thought, and such pretty gold paper!"

"It's all gone."

Her face sagged. Did Jocelyn seriously think I'd eaten everything myself? The gold paper I'd folded away. For a moment I considered—no. She'd just thank me and thank me. I moved on to other conversations.

Of the four women now berating me, two claimed that *the least I could have done* was to hand over that pretty paper.

Another said, "Jocelyn deserved that basket."

"I didn't? Was it an award for merit, then?"

As expected, she had no answer.

The last intervenor opined that giving *poor Jossy* either paper or basket would only have shown additional contempt.

I reminded them all of the familiar phrase, *luck of the draw.*

The four exchanged *She's hopeless* glances. (We've all known each other for decades through our jobs and/or political sympathies, cultural interests—the social-connective tissue shared by elderly women alone for this reason or that.) Then they eyed my raspberry thumbprints and almond slices, and each took another. Their next agenda item: Geraldine.

Like me, at the hospital thrift store where we volunteer, Geraldine prefers spending time with the used books to arranging second-hand clothes that were ugly even when new. Our book section's busy. With so many real bookstores closing in Vancouver, we get callers and buyers from across the city.

Unlike me, Geraldine chats at length with customers, natters about authors' marriages and addictions and feuds. She forgets titles, mixes up who wrote what, and can't manage the computer. At the cash register, people get near-frantic, trying to pay and escape. I make sure to answer the phone.

Recently, a peevish Englishman called. In search of a particular *Inspector Morse*, he'd got the runaround from a big-box store.

That very day I'd sold the title he sought to a quick reader. "It'll be back soon. I'd advise you to call again next week."

"A pleasure to deal with someone efficient. Do I detect an English accent?"

Those who ask this—and many do, for, in spite of Asian immigration in recent decades, the Brit infestation endures here—have no interest in me. They want a fix of nostalgia. I, having spent one boring year with an English aunt five decades ago, have none to indulge.

"No."

"Then my thanks again. May I have your name?"

"Geraldine. I'm in every Tuesday." Enjoyable falsehood.

"I'll stop by."

Two pests at once!

The intervenors, cookies in hand, confirmed that Geraldine and Mr Nosy Peevish hadn't enjoyed their meeting.

"At your age, Edith, you shouldn't play pranks like that."

"When, then?"

No answer to that either.

After I refreshed their cups, the four ran out their biggest gun.

Months ago, Lillian had offered to pick me up at six and drive me to a constituency meeting. At five-fifty I was in my lobby, ready. At ten past the hour, impatient. At fifteen, heading for one bus, then another, in a downpour.

Agenda and minutes had already been adopted by the time I arrived. Quickly I took a chair at the back. Lillian sat near the front. When I rose to speak on a motion, her head snapped round. Horrified, her look. Hand at her mouth.

All through the break, I talked with our treasurer and secretary. Lillian couldn't get at me till adjournment, when we all crowded to gather umbrellas and coats.

Her hand again rose, to shield her spluttering lips. "Edith! So *so* sorry, how careless of me! How could I?" Etc.

"It's all right." Not far from true. Inconvenience, yes, and annoyance, but not disaster. Still, I was glad that neighbours had offered me a ride home, so I could decline her strenuous offer.

Later that week Lillian's handwritten note arrived, reiterating all that she'd said at the meeting. To answer: redundant, surely.

Soon we met again, at a fundraising dinner. Her eyes, wide as before. Her grimace perhaps slighter. Briefly, fingers to lips.

"*So* sorry! I still feel so bad!"

I demurred, gestured towards the jovial emcee taking the stage.

That was surely the end of the matter?

No. At the opera, at political meetings and work parties and book club, Lillian and I repeatedly met. Every time, the startle. The facial twitch. The hand rising—not as high now, only chest-level. Vestigial gestures, codified.

"Sorry!" Still audible.

I didn't respond—yet Lillian's grovelling drove me to reconsider her original proposal of a lift. *Her* proposal. I never ask for rides. First I'd waited for her, and then in rain I'd stood waiting for two buses.

The publicity of lateness, as it were, the inevitable group awareness that personal disorder (of whatever kind) has disrupted a process—I dislike that.

As for Lillian's look when she heard my voice at the meeting.... Well. If in advance she'd considered the agenda, had thought about who might argue what, she'd not imagined Edith in the room. Her generous impulse (did it ever exist?) had been satisfied by making the offer. Fulfillment wasn't required.

One evening at the theatre, as intermission began I glimpsed Lillian heading for the bar. I got to the lineup first. Without looking, I sensed her cringing stance behind me. Yes, I could have forgone my glass of wine, but why should I? Why not she?

After ordering, I turned to give her what she wanted. "You behaved badly to me, Lillian. I haven't forgotten." Merlot in hand, I walked off.

By now my coffee pot was empty, my platter held only one almond slice, and my four friends wanted me to tell Lillian I was sorry.

"She made an empty gesture. I called her on it. What's the problem?"

Unable to say, they departed my home frowning.

I ate the last slice and cleaned up my kitchen, asking myself who was the person inconvenienced, forgotten? Edith. Who was targeted by unjustified envy, harassed by nattering and nosiness, burdened by fawning apologies? Edith. Why should Edith apologize? I ask you, why?

HISTORY LESSON(S)

2009

Like everyone my age, I contain a young foreigner. Not totally strange, on the beach back there as the waves crash, but now my prostate's doubled, belly tripled. Ears and libido droop, knees refuse, teeth rattle, bionic eyes and bald head glitter. Too often, the mind's engine moves on long-laid rails.

In 1977 I *observed* that fewer new people, contacts as we on the far left called them, turned up for demos, forums, marches. Brilliant, Harold! Half-sighted, I also typified radicals worldwide in *not inferring* that rebellion's king tide was on the ebb.

Today, who'll keep the book's deathwatch with me?

People talk of new modalities, although for books, now, *new* and *used* are irrelevant categories. Duthie's empire gone. Women In Print, gone. R2B2, Octopus, Magpie, Pauline's, long gone. McNally-Robinson, near bankrupt. Coles and W H Smith, colonized. McLeod's still stands downtown, along with Criterion, Albion. My store's an East Side outlier.

Half-blindness marked much of my earlier life.

Take a look.

November–December 1977

When Harold learns he's to be acting organizer of the Vancouver branch, his nose bleeds. He stretches out on the sofa, head a-dangle, unable to chair the Sunday meeting though all the executive sit ready. Congrats aren't in order, because rifts in the International and in Canada mean no one important will assume the role.

Today Comrade Myrna, asst organizer, will chair. And take minutes, which Cde Diana won't, on women's liberation principles. Her plump panty-hosed thighs hiss when she shifts in her chair. None of the men knows shorthand.

Now, questions on Harold's treasurer's report.

"Why are we in the red, comrade?"

His voice snuffles through blood. "We spent more than we took in." He fumbles in a pocket for toilet paper.

"Don't be funny!"

"I'm not, Myrna. Membership's down."

Diana frowns. "*I* bring contacts around!"

"Enough, Diana."

Myrna herds them through a proposed longshore contract. They analyse a recent NDP constituency meeting, choose forum speakers, endorse an equal-pay demo. Harold takes the movement's tabloid out of his briefcase, longs instead for Conan Doyle, waiting there just as Ambler did in high school.

"All in favour any opposed carried," says Myrna, again.

Harold tucks bloody twists behind a cushion. Slowly, the nostril dries but his head stays down. He lowers the newspaper over his crotch.

"No New Business. Adjourned."

"Wait!" Harold sits up. "Fusion?"

"Discussion's deferred, to January." Myrna waves a letter. "From Centre."

As Harold grabs it, red drops fall.

Most of the others leave to escort Doug, ex-organizer, to the airport for ascension to Centre in Toronto. Harold's not invited. With the spotty letter he heads for now-sort-of-his office, a beaverboard cubicle, shoulder-height, in dim rented revolutionary space that rises way way up.

Lying on the floor, nose plugged, he reads the letter from Centre. Puzzles, rereads. Why does the leadership stall on the long-promoted move to fuse with another Trotskyist group?

The door opens. Myrna.

"Busy, I see." Leers at him.

Her flat behind doesn't interest Harold. His own's fat, hateful. He envisions Beth, a contact whose lovely hair he'd noticed on a march to the US Embassy. At the Georgia Street turn, the floating strands met the wind and blew about. She laughed, didn't try to contain them. Did she glance his way during the forum on Quebec independence? She's with Myrna, Diana, in a CR group. Can a man mention that? What *is* CR, anyway?

Enough.

"Myrna, remember at UBC how anti-war collapsed over stupid disagreements on small things? Fusion's *necessary*."

"*Deferred*. Tidy up, organizer!"

She spills some paper clips, leaves.

Scowling, Harold checks his nose. Inserts another tissue, in case, and rises to survey the desk: piled folders, loose-leaf, white typescript, yellow carbons, purple dittos, Gestetnered pages, newsprint. Similar detritus tops each file cabinet. Papers crowd the shelves, protrude between volumes of *Britannica*'s 1927 edition containing, in *Lan-Mu*, Trotsky's entry on Lenin.

From now till the Fusion debate, Harold has six weeks to sift sort organize decades of paper. He visualizes basic tabs, knows that sub- and sub-sub-heads will evolve.

Four-thirty. He unwraps a Mars Bar. Begins.

Goes home at ten.

Nine a.m. Monday, he's back.

At ten-thirty, time for Oh Henry.

Diana enters. No knock. Black pantyhose.

"Harold! What will *you* do about the dirty old men?"

"Huh?"

"Don't pretend! *Duncan*."

"What? I'm not."

"Duncan sits way too close at socials. *Leers*. I have to move! George and Henry, same. We're all sick of so-called radicals looking up our dresses."

Harold wonders, *But aren't all those men old?*

"Doug did nothing. *You* talk to them."

He touches his nose, hopeful.

"I'll do it with you. Beth and Sandra too."

"But they're not comrades! Only contacts!"

"We're *women,* insulted in this hall." Her breasts shake.

"Diana, I have to get to school."

She rises, legs hissing. "You have to *act*, Harold."

Leaves.

From the alley behind the Hall, he fetches a trash can. Eager to file revolutionary socialism, today he'll skip two classes in his college Office Admin program. He gets all As, and since childhood he's known order. At home, clothes hung by function. Interior doors stayed shut, toilets lidded.

Excavating cabinets, Harold handles coloured tabs, typed labels that speak of long-ago efforts. Other assignments overtook those earlier comrades, but he's now got the time, authority, and skill to create a filing system that *works*.

Noon. One more drawer.

More bulging folders, their tabs soft, crumpled. The purple dittos often smear when fresh, and with regret Harold dumps handfuls of unintelligible history. Grabs another. What's this?

Handwritten. Ruled yellow sheets. Undated. Bright staples. The signature, familiar. Ex-organizer Doug can't spell—yet here's a clear plan for a secret faction. First, stall the Fusion debate, to raise internal eagerness and, to the other group, suggest weakness. In January, resume discussion. Ensure passage at the May plenum. Then *Take power, get rid of them.*

Simple dimple. Harold tucks the letter in his briefcase, alongside Holmes' *Adventures*, and heads out towards the bus, the college, Business English, and Cobol.

That night, after KD and instant pudding, he tapes Doug's doc to his bathroom mirror, by *Memos to self* about soap, Metamucil. Brushing, he re-peruses.

If this faction's real, who's in it? Does Myrna know? Did she type a final version? Or did the plan fly to Centre in Doug's head?

Before bed he reads Holmes at length, sleeps poorly. Same, the next night. The next, a nosebleed rouses Harold, and staunching it fractures sleep for good.

How to launder bloody bed-linen? He's never "lived" with a girl, a woman, nor did his home permit red manifestations of femaleness. In all weathers Mum slipped outside to the bin, wrapped packet in hand. His sister, too.

Now Mandy's a Jehovah's Witness. Do JW women do that? On his dresser, her grad photo smiles. He hates Dad's tears, Mum's rages. In that house, did a red-spotted sheet ever *happen*? Sperm's nearly colourless, but Mum surely saw.

Midweek, Diana's rarely at the hall. Therefore, Harold the acting organizer does nothing about the alleged misogyny of Duncan, George, Henry. Nothing.

He files. He studies Cobol, like Marxism a code alive and working globally though visible to few.

As Friday's public forum nears, however, his anxiety rises.

Harold explains to Myrna, who's arranging chairs.

"*Last Sunday* Diana told you this? Here."

He sets out leaflets. "Duncan doesn't realize he's rude. Those men all just admire Diana. She brings contacts around."

"Oh, everyone admires *her*." Myrna nears. "Set up a meeting, Harold. I'll write a script. We'll prepare together!"

He breathes Rothmans, unwashed skin. Blurts, "No."

Withdraws. For two days, fakes a cold. Then obeys Myrna. Phones everyone. Maybe no one will show?

No such luck. Here's Beth, whose twining hair glistens. She's hand-in-hand with Sandra. He didn't know. Wonders, shamed, why they'd care about old geezers' eyes.

Next come Myrna, Diana, silent, stern.

George's hearing is, as he often says, not getting any better.

So that Henry's good eye can focus, he sits at an angle to the group crowded into sort-of-Harold's office.

Duncan's grasped that the women are upset, not why. He smiles at Diana. "You're looking handsome today, comrade!"

"See what I mean? Pig!" Screams, an inch from his face.

Duncan's tears start, the thin seep of age.

Henry shouts, "Bitch!"

"Fucking chauvinists!" Sandra.

Beth's wide-eyed, alarmed.

After Henry's explained, George growls, "I wouldn't touch one of 'em with a ten-foot pole."

Sandra issues loud variations on *Never darken this door again*, stamps out. Beth follows.

"Comrades," Harold pleads, "sit down, talk this through?"

Just as with Dad when he issued commands, no one obeys. Alone, he unwraps Aero and files.

He files as December moves on. Myrna and Diana avoid him, George and Henry too. Duncan's still chatty. Harold introduces speakers, reviews accounts, has the Shop-Vac fixed, orders silk-screen ink. Files. Chains a long-distance logbook to the desk, though comrades don't reliably enter their calls.

At home, he's sick of the now-curling yellow letter.

Show Myrna? No, Doug likely changed his mind, so it's best if only Harold's shocked. Keep it in his briefcase? When taking out Velveeta sandwiches, he'd sense it daily. Toss, burn, eat the doc? He can't do that to an archive.

Hide it in the office? *Britannica!* Not the *Lan-Mu* vol. Into *Dar-Ed* slides the yellow sheet.

Harold sleeps better. Magical thinking for sure, to "prevent" contact between Trotsky/Lenin and Doug, but who cares? Filing's pleasure now quells his urge to reread. His new system's sound, streamlined for radicals aboard this period's roller coaster of reverses, successes, reverses.

January–February 1978

Documents from all Canadian branches arrive for the Fusion debate. On every lumpy springless couch, comrades read, smoke, argue. (One hunts a pencil, finds rusty twists behind a cushion.)

Harold organizes special meetings. Each doc needs a supporter (possibly genuine) to present it, and an opponent (ditto), before general debate. For him, invisible and inaudible wording doubles each text, speech.

A doc under Myrna's party name takes a pro-Fusion stance. She's verbose (Harold's writing instructor stresses concision), but comrades respond, laugh at her jokes. That *Britannica* plan wasn't funny, though. Wasn't shaped by a nobody.

One February evening, with Myrna and Harold alone at the Hall, she barges in with a Gestetnered sheet.

"Slipped under the front door, just now."

Whatever typewriter produced this letter's stencil had a capital T out of alignment. Harold reads *he rots have infiltrated our CR group, and we as womyn will not have our space contaminated by rotskyite male values.* This line of thought continues down the page to *he rot women must go.* Unsigned, undated.

The ceiling light fails.

Myrna and Harold fetch bulbs, a ladder. He climbs, loathing his weight. Unscrews 100-watts, shakes them, hears bulb death.

"Diana'd have a fit," says Myrna in the dim, "and then make excuses for Beth and Sandra. Like always."

"You won't show her the letter?"

"No way! I'll hide it, here maybe. Handle those two myself."

Harold hesitates. Is this a test? An invitation?

In goes the new bulb. After only a moment's illumination, he sees Myrna select *Dar-Edu.* He'd left that volume sticking out a bit.

"How'd you get this letter?"

Nosebleed's imminent.

"No one but us was supposed to see it!"

Red splashes on curved grey glass.

"Who's *us*, Myrna?"

She shakes the ladder.

"Stop! I'll expose the faction!" Red drops fly.

Shake. "No you won't, Harold! You didn't even tell me! Intractably petty bourgeois. Our leadership *wants* this, the International too."

He throws the dead bulb, she dodges. Scrambling down, he rushes for toilet paper. On his return, Myrna, Doug's letter, and the womyn's doc have all disappeared. Supine, Harold waits not to bleed.

2009

Three decades later—grief.

Shame.

Embarrassment about Metamucil, my life's companion.

Disgust? Too strong (except for the candy).

Annoyance at my ineradicable tendency to lard prose with qualifiers, parentheses, lists. Does admiration sift through sarcasm? Too close, can't see. Nostalgia I've tried to kill.

Those nosebleeds. The doc said cauterization, I heard castration. My prescription, simple: *Do nothing. Repeat as needed. Hope.*

Our parents prayed Mandy'd quit her cult to be their mild girl again; later, that she'd get off street drugs, out of Riverview. They *acted*. I only hoped that Diana's anger would fade, Beth seduce me,

Myrna vanish. That as organizer I'd face no political demands. Just serve. Not lead.

Difficult still, admitting youth's ignorance!

I quote: *Duncan doesn't realize*. What did I know of older men's desires? Those of my peers, even my own, bewildered me. The few women I'd slept with didn't return my calls. Why? I *hoped*. Hope: sure recipe for refusal to change.

Duncan went with the Mac-Paps to Spain, though his rambling anecdotes taught me little of that war. For years he frequented my bookstore, to talk politics and kindly buy Tey, Crofts, Allingham, Sayers. At ninety, a hospital death. No war could offer worse. Never dotty, though. With my dad, Beth helped so much.

George with Henry survived the Shachtman-Burnham fight in the Socialist Workers' Party. Henry collected hardboiled—no, I digress. Protesting Vietnam, they both quit the US for "British" Columbia. Most comrades, like me, didn't *see* a gay pair seeking a home less hostile than Texas. Amazing, the still-deep closets of the 70s. Also amazing, straight radicals' indifference.

The CR group, including Beth, expelled my comrades.

In spite of Myrna's factional deceit over the Fusion debate, in spite of Diana's quitting the 4-I in hopes of readmission to that conscious-raising group (nix), they're still political sisters. And friends. Mine too. We're alone now.

Diana went through lovers like a hot knife. Never chose. Got fat. (We diet together, up down up.) Still pretty, for years she's run a consignment shop, Perfect Plus, her clientele largely (ha ha) from Kerrisdale and Point Grey.

Annually, PP holds a Fresh Dress gala for women in the Downtown Eastside.

Myrna's still thin plain pushy. After the Turn To Industry in '78, she spent years on the green-chain, then moved sideways into union politics. Up up up. Speaks well, dresses well. A great reader—she found Mankell for me.

In her late fifties, the NDP offered a provincial nomination.

"I declined," giggling. "A Trot couldn't keep a straight face!"

Myrna has a good pension. Diana'll manage, when she sells. Me? Who'd want a book-hoard? Fat guardian dragon, I'll die atop my valueless treasure. Never retire! Never exercise or meditate! *Do nothing. Repeat as needed.*

Sisterly, M and D remonstrate with and laugh at me.

Every autumn we host a dinner for the Rev. Our guests? Careful! Some old Trots only speak bitterness betrayal blah blah, but others enjoy reminiscence, feel safe to theorize about splits, turns, line-changes, the RCMP payroll. Once we invited two social dems plus a CP colleague in the book trade, but the ambience was off. So, just us. A dozen? George, Henry, long gone. Duncan outlived them.

Who are *we*, the far-left diaspora of the 70s, 80s? *Community activists* often, though working with other aging sectarians feels peculiar because each knows exactly how the other's group shattered, rotted. What we do seems at best modestly helpful. Also, though young rebellion greened with the Gulf War and Afghanistan, it's shrivelled again.

Still, our cohort lost less than the hard left leftover from the 1950s, 40s, 30s. Phone trees, lifelong friendships, public roles—a civilization, really—vanished with the soup kettle that fed sixty and the sense of historical purpose.

For me, disorder took power when print gave way.

My young foreigner won't admit our store's only storage, awaiting the landfill. He *arranges* actual books, I use the Cobol-filled computer. Uneven development. I don't know when I lost my parents' faith, why I keep mine, or when I first found Holmes, dreamed of a bookstore, knew that a mystery's best part is the puzzling middle. I remember Beth's illness. Mandy's. I remember a teenager who opened an early Paretsky in my store and, sighing, set it down. "Too expensive."

I'll carry used books too! Recognition of necessity.

Back again. Take another look.

1972–1978

In his third year, Harold took a course on French Indochina. (It happened to fit his schedule. An hour earlier/later, another story?) His research on imperialism shocked him. After acing the exam, he found UBC's main concourse full of demonstrators. Protests against the American invasion of Vietnam hadn't previously drawn his notice.

A girl handed him a leaflet. He read.

Asked, "Can I carry a placard?"

She shoved a bucket at him. "First get donations."

Ask permission. Obey. Familiar. His bucket soon full of cash, Harold held a placard and shouted.

Myrna mentioned a forum at a Trotskyist hall. He went. Again. At rallies and meetings, observed the comrades' skills. Admired. Participated, studied, listened. After a month, joined the 4-I. Combined development! Membership didn't feel optional, nor did quitting post-secondary for politics.

"How'd we go wrong-g-g?" Mum's teeth. "Not another red cent from us."

Harold waited on ever more tables, assigning his big tips to higher party dues and to savings. Otherwise, he struggled.

Intractably serious, he'd gobbled the sweet far-left lingo, *position, mass action, infantile disorder, unprincipled*. All trades have their tongues, yes, but in '73 he couldn't even giggle at the movement headline, *Hands Off Wounded Knee!* (Now I laugh till it hurts.) He never saw why marchers raising the banner *Stop the War in Vietnam!* mustn't go near another worded almost the same.

After the Yanks fled Saigon, he entered college. Way cheaper. Revolutionary life continued, routine, till the fake organizer status fell upon him.

Reaching January 1978 brought Harold relief, for again Mandy'd refused to celebrate the abomination of Christmas. Dad wept, Mum excoriated. Could they, back in their unknowable youth, have imagined such suffering? Other difficulties that the New Year might resolve included the debate, Harold's nose, Diana's anger, Myrna's desire. The faction remained unutterable.

A leisurely coastal spring began as he paid, fixed, ordered, chaired, filed. Reeled back from Djikstra's line, "Cobol cripples the mind," but recovered.

Saw a nose-man. Who named a date.

May. Though writing finals, Harold attended the branch meeting when the BC delegation reported on the Toronto plenum. Myrna held the gavel. Success for Fusion!

At the specialist's office, he smelled his seared, healed flesh, then sought caffeine and sugar in a nearby cafe.

Beth sat alone, reading a mystery.

"Oh Harold!"

Side-by-side, for fifteen years.

The faction took power. Got rid. The Canadian movement bled out, at first in noisy resignations and expulsions. Then silence. Comrades just quit coming. Harold wouldn't do that. Was that action? Myrna had to accuse him of plotting, and call a vote.

2009

Duncan and I chewed over the Hydra-headed Marxist term *Bonapartist*.

One definition: *a grotesque mediocrity* reprises a hero's part, so tragedy repeats as farce.

Another: if neither contending force can win, someone, to prevent disintegration, assumes power's mask. An unwitting wearer, I got the revolutionary boot. Farewell, filing system! Among my best, youthful triumph unequalled later, etc.

I did act, when I could. After George Henry Duncan backed me, after Beth discovered our storefront, after I began full-time ordering shelving selling books, I engineered secret visits with my sister. She and my Beth met. Happiness!

Then Mandy got disfellowshipped, which meant still more time together, all three of us, though by then we'd buried Mum and Dad.

Another tragedy, farce, huge, tiny, what you will.

RABBIT, BIRD, YARROW

A rabbit leapt up from the beach and through the high grass, scattering dew into the morning. Stopped.

Because they'd drawn breath? blinked?

Silent. Invisible, but one flower on a tall stem swayed. So, the animal, hidden right there. Scared? Just checking?

Another jump, one long ear forward, one back. A bright brown eye. The fur's delicate ticking, its sheen.

Down again. Pause. Then a rustle. Gone, into thick salal under the firs.

The couple smiled, grateful for this rabbit on their last day of such pleasant play-time, also grateful for the pretty steep-sided valley that held the lake, and for June's gentle warmth, not July's swelter. Another gift to retirees: a campground minus noisy school-age kids.

Their breakfast kettle sounded. They ate local honey, early blueberries, and poured coffee just as that boy rode by their site on his first morning circuit.

How old? About four, Mark and Stacy thought, remembering.

Sturdy, in plaid shirt and denim shorts. A purposeful look. Stones and lumpy roots studded the trail, but he hardly needed the training wheels on his little bike. Shy. After multiple meetings he still didn't say *Hi* back, so now the couple just smiled, waved.

Exploring, they'd seen him at a high-domed tent featuring a spacious vestibule. A new SUV stood nearby. On Mum's lap, a smaller boy grinned up at her. Two-ish? Dad managed a full-size barbecue.

Parental directives, familiar, reached Stacy's and Mark's ears. At meals sometimes they heard a sob, or wail, then Dad's loud voice.

"Don't do that! I said, Stop it!"

At the beach, dreamy Two just sat in the water, lifting and dropping pebbles, laughing at each splash. Dad read. Four swam hard, attended by Mum. His dog-paddle strengthened.

So—what might this couple, Mark and Stacy, do today?

Discussion ended as on each lovely morning to date. Hike round the lake, find lunch in the village. Nap, then swim or rent a canoe. Wander the loop trails' dappled shade, cool and dust-free, till time came for food, campfire, Scrabble, stars, sleep. Tomorrow, back to the city.

In late afternoon, walking in the second-growth forest, again they encountered plaid-shirted Four on his bike.

Two ran delightedly alongside his brother, pumping his arms. Such a smile! His tummy stuck out, baby-like, above tiny blue Y-fronts. He stopped to gaze in wonder at the old strangers.

Four met their eyes also.

"My brother doesn't have any clothes on."

Stacy and Mark cried, "He's fine!" "What a good runner!"

The little one smiled, and both boys went on.

The couple walked longer than usual in the woods, silent until the trail crossed an old logging road. Which way?

"Doesn't matter."

"You don't give a shit?"

"I didn't say that!"

"Your tone did."

Back at their site, the spat continued, until they started on wine and dinner.

Discussion. How could such a young child feel that shamed need to apologize? To them? As for that boy's parents, what had they taught him? In a western country, in this new century? What went on in that expensive tent? Etc.

Stacy and Mark poured another glass, took more food. They'd nearly reached *And why does this event upset us so?* when Dad's volume rose through the trees.

"Don't *do* that! *Bad* boys!"

A child, children, wailing.

Admonishment, in Mum's low tone.

Quiet.

The couple then reminisced about how they themselves were shamed as kids. Not new tales, these—shared years ago after the first awkward dates, as they got to know each other, really know—but produced as relevant now.

A child's high cry. "I don't *like* it, Da-dee!"

Oh such a shuddering bang! A fist, slamming on the picnic table? No shout. Was Dad's face-close-up, scary? Whispering, threatening?

"But I don't want to eat that stuff, I do-o-o-n't!"

Again bang. The wood, reverberating, drew a faint echo from the hillside.

Tears, diminuendo.

In the lengthening silence, did other campers also consider ambling past that site, maybe, en route to the bathhouse or the bear-proof steel garbage bin, just to see if anything...?

Stacy and Mark stayed put. Considered their own practices with their own children, long ago.

Perfect parents? Of course not. Mark admitted to poor handling of his son's early encounters with drugs and sex. His wife had criticized his approach, Stacy recalled, and whatever else might be said of that woman she wasn't stupid.

Stacy herself had failed "miserably," as she always put it, at mothering her teenage daughter. "Miserably!" Her man? More hindrance than help.

"Must you go on about him again? I've heard it all."

"If you don't *mind*, I'll just mention that he and I have a grandchild somewhere. Whom we'll never see, never know."

Mark grunted.

Chopping wood for kindling, he attacked Stacy's solidarity with her ex. She'd stayed way too long, been so damaged. The daughter still thought the guy was great, too. What a waste. Not that Mark said that, ever.

Stacy, contemplating the loser and jerk that his son had grown into, washed the supper dishes. Sad really. Mark had tried his best to help, still tried, deserved better. All that money. After each visit, he needed days to recover.

Down the lake, a loon cried. The two smiled. *We're so lucky!* The first night they'd heard hoots, checked their bird book by flashlight. Not a screech, of that they were sure, and since then they'd not heard that cry. Now sitting close, beside their fire, they remembered how today the morning rabbit hid by a flower.

Their field guide? Here, yes here, and the *White* section showed, that's it, a creamy lacy blossom. Yarrow. Perfect.

In the semi-dark, a sudden wail.

Pause for breath, another wail, then full screams, howls. "Noooo Daddy, don't, noooooo!"

Roaring, "Shit's everywhere, goddammit! Never do that again!"

Ain, softly from the hill.

Mum shrieked, "For fuck's sake, you asshole!"

Sssso.

The sobs developed wider separations. Ceased.

In the quiet, Stacy whispered, "She's at the end of her tether."

And who tethered her? Mark didn't ask, spoke at normal volume. "Myself, I wouldn't take a two-year-old camping."

Stacy got up and stepped away so as not to slap his face, stepped back and sat down so as not to run to that unknown mother.

As their fire shrank they didn't play Scrabble, though a tournament was their camping tradition. Giggling at themselves, they'd kept all their scores, and after ten years were pretty even. This trip, each had won three games.

On their cosy camp-bed they had to lie close. Didn't dare touch.

No owl.

Tomorrow: strike the tent, pack up the car. For hours they'd take equal turns at the wheel, passing by mountains, pastureland, and bright quick creeks, yarrow in the ditches, all beautiful, all fun except the inescapable traffic through drab suburbs. Then there they'd be, back inside their plate-glass waterfront view, inside their own, their own whatever it was.

Mark, waking around three, left the tent as quietly as he could.

Blackness. Gradual shape, contour. A dark blue sky, sweet air, near-silence. Those little boys invisible. Asleep. Like his own son. Presumably.

While peeing, Mark reviewed his well-curated list of *If onlys*. For a long time after meeting Stacy he'd thought happiness might dissolve that pain, but it stayed separate and hard as each lakeside stone.

Back to bed—and the flannelette on Stacy's side held no warmth.

Go out to find her? Wait?

Wait.

With care she'd managed the steep, rooty path down to the beach where the water sipped, sipped. Crying, Stacy tried to keep her sobs even quieter than that. How long since she'd touched her girl? Heard her voice, even by phone?

She'd crawl through that expensive tent's vestibule, shake the Dad hard. *Nothing ever, ever will hurt you so much,* she'd say. *Control yourself, buster!*

Back to bed, where Mark lay still. Stacy settled. Hush, hush, silent as the rabbit, two hands clasped so tight they felt the sharpness of each other's nails. A whisper. "Tomorrow, breakfast in the village before we go?"

"Yes! Those great pancakes."

Roused by the earth's turning, a bird spoke. Not an owl.

OPEN, CLOSE

My darling girl, I feel strangely that I might die quite soon, so I am writing to you.

As I hunted on Mum's messy desk for paper clips, this slipped into view, a page torn from her notebook about houses she was selling. Her scrawl. Was that word *strongly?*

You are almost thirteen now [wrong, almost fifteen], *old enough to understand. My absence will be hard for you, but you are strong and will manage. Know that your Daddy loves you dearly, though he doesn't always show it. He will do his best. Always remember he will be deeply sad. My pals have known and loved you since your birth and will do all they can. You can speak openly to them about anything* [the last word underlined thrice]. *Dearest Eleanor, do wash your hair regularly, and your whole self. You are not always fastidious, nor completely honest. With boys, be careful not...*

Loathsome, each word. Of course my mother put F's needs first, even if imaginary. When didn't she? As for talking to her "pals," awful old slang, about anything of significance—grotesque. What boys? And not one word about boring Aunt Kay. Did Mum intend me to find this? Two years unfinished, yet kept? Forgotten? Stupid. I shoved it deep into the midden by her typewriter, left a note. *I need paper clips!* Why didn't she let F give her an electric? Stupid.

Back in my own room, I couldn't not think of that letter.

Sentimentalizing, self-dramatizing—if I knew those terms, they didn't come to mind. What hit me: the tone. Often I'd imagine what I might have said to a teacher, or a bullying girl at school, or to angry F. These polished speeches I silently recited, racing fantasies of victory till the horses fell over and died. Was Mum doing that? Could she be that dumb? Death? She never got sick, unlike F, always complaining full-bore, stomach, back, knees, eyes, etc.

"*I'm* healthy as a hog," she'd laugh, brewing tea for him.

"Lucy, don't talk like a farmer!"

More laughter. "I did grow up in the country, remember?"

"I don't like it."

Yes, healthy my mother was, lively, with a flair for making connections. She sold real estate part-time (F's manly pride in his successful office-supplies business wouldn't tolerate more), always imagining how *this* unique client might live in *that* space. She read multiple novels at once, left them about on chairs. Sweaters too, earrings, her purse.

"Oh Lucy!" F put these objects away.

With vigour Mum gossiped, gardened. She drove her Nash Rambler the same way, so the pals nicknamed her Left-Hand Lu for the daring with which she made such turns.

F imagined, therefore, when the news came, that his Lucy had dared too greatly. No. Some stupid driver blasted through a stop sign, T-boning the Nash.

Gone.

Gone, on February first. I'd read that draft in mid-January.

During the post-funeral reception at our house, a gnarled man ate several devilled eggs. Two women, old, inspecting me, whispered, "So like Lu! And your dear granny. Lucky she didn't live to see this day."

F snarled, "Kay, get those goddamned people out of here."

She complied.

Who? Who cared? A sole child, no available grandparents, I knew only my aunt as extended family.

To get through the dreadful rites, I'd obsessed about clothes and food. Run the washer and wringer, hang things in the chill basement, iron them—those tasks I could do. Not F's shirts. Weekly, Mum drove to a Chinese laundry that "did" them properly, then to the supermarket. I was too young to drive. F's license had lapsed; her turquoise convertible took him everywhere. Only one fresh shirt waited in his closet.

The mourners gone, Aunt Kay warmed up the homemade soup she'd brought for a light supper. I decided not to mention the shirt predicament to her. Telling F never crossed my mind. Mum's housekeeping allowance awaited, in a coffee-can. I'd manage. I'd do everything.

Heading upstairs, I heard my aunt open the fridge.

"You'll be all right till the weekend. I'll take her shopping then."

"*I'll be all right?* How can you, Kay?"

I closed my door.

Young people now must feel invisible too, for teenagers walk blindly reading through crowds, traffic. Discovering other hominids close by, they startle. I, one day post-funeral, having traversed thirty blocks while dragging the bundle-buggy plus carrying the rack of shirts, got home in my bizarre, no, my ridiculous school uniform just as all the street's fathers returned from work.

Two shirts were creased. "Unwearable." Also I'd bought the wrong grind of coffee and broken an egg. That evening my headmistress, her class sensibilities affronted by my expedition, telephoned F. He activated Aunt Kay. No longer could I nobly, solitarily play my new role.

At school I'd missed tests in algebra, Elizabethan history, so now my facsimile wrote them in empty classrooms. While I cried, she also translated from/to various languages, living, dead. At home she took out the garbage, set letters of condolence on F's desk, spoke awkwardly to the cleaning-woman whom the pals had insisted be hired. And prepared meals.

For weeks after the death, food offerings arrived on our front porch.

F rejected all casseroles. "Your mother never made muck like this." We ate the baked goods (enraging proof of his faked digestive problems), tossed the rest. Not all donors identified themselves, though, and few claimed their cookware. Who owned this flowered platter? I dreaded to seem a fool. "Um, did you bring the lamb stew?" I hid Corningware on upper kitchen shelves. What would Mum say?

We also appeared in other dining rooms, as guests of kind neighbours and of F's business partners. Heavy companions, I'd imagine now, incapable of table talk. On our departure, soon (I had homework, we couldn't bear it any longer), our hostess would hand me some baked ham or apple crumble. I wasn't grateful. I just liked these foods, both in themselves and as solutions to next day's dinner. Soon F decided, though, that such gifts signified charity. Half-smiling, he made the *Stop!* sign, a deprecating refusal.

Of course he and I returned no invitations.

What would I have served? All winter we'd endured one of F's convictions that his insides had gone horribly wrong, so he, we, must eat only *the plainest of plain food*. At table I sat between my parents, F on my left. (That ear, always chilly.) MWF, baked fish, frozen peas, baked potatoes. TTS, poached chicken, frozen beans, boiled potatoes. Applesauce then, trickled with maple syrup.

(Once when I was small, a winter drive to "the country," to fields pale blue with snow. A barn. F stayed in the car. Cow-smell. I got a cookie. Mum's woolly glove pulled mine. I held a big metal container of sweetness, cold. F's voice, grating. *Why did you pay for that? They're poor. You owe those people nothing, Lucy. Not after what... Hush.*)

Most Sundays, we three went to Aunt Kay's tiny apartment.

"I can't eat this," said F, no matter what.

"For you, little brother, I mashed the spuds with skim. Eat up!"

Mum's eyes beheld her plate. How did my aunt Kay make F behave? He even ate a small second helping of beef.

Later, Mum might say, "Good-quality beef isn't cheap. Your sister pinches, for you."

F frowned. "By definition, a single legal secretary pinches."

Mum sighed.

"Remember, Lucy, I didn't tell Kay to refuse the opportunities that came her way. Nor did I introduce her to Mr B."

"Hush!"

Our pre-death menu, after donations ceased, continued until I dared to try some of Mum's cookbooks. Success eluded me. After one dinner of burned cheese sauce and bullet meatballs, next day I set plain old potatoes and fish in the oven, returning to Latin with relief. I even remembered to set a timer.

F found me in tears before a stone-cold oven. *Mum would know what to do*, I didn't say. Nor did he. We ignoramuses turned knobs, toggled switches. F knelt to peer under the stove.

"Dead," he said. Looking up, "Stop crying. We'll go out."

Today I live downtown, where restaurants of twenty nationalities crowd my neighbourhood, wafting deliciousness outward. Often I dine with friends, but back then F might as well have said, "We'll have dinner on the moon."

We rode the streetcar to Murray's. Such elegance! A menu in italics, the waitresses in pastel caps and aprons, scalloped like the paper place mats. I imagine now the women's sturdy, white shoes, their girdles, the bras with multiple hooks-and-eyes. Slips, of course.

F ordered lemonade (my glass sugar-crusted), and red wine.

What did we eat? Not baked fish, not poached chicken.

F described the principles of offset printing. I asked questions, he answered. We ate. The silences didn't hurt. I didn't count my chews, didn't as at home calculate the minutes till I could get up to occupy myself in the kitchen, so grateful to be done with him.

Then we took a taxi. Another astonishment.

"Bedtime now." F kissed me. "Homework? Don't worry. Tomorrow I'll telephone Miss Whatsit. Eleanor?"

I turned.

"We had a good evening, didn't we?" Wet eyes. Smiling.

I went on upstairs.

Now other agents earned Mum's commissions. Weekly, Aunt Kay did the shirts-and-groceries run with me. The house-cleaner cleaned. F hired a gardener, took streetcars, buses, taxis.

Mum's pals talked about her, instead of with her. (Years later I wept at Auden's line about dead Yeats, *He became his admirers.*) One pal, a nurse, drew diagrams showing how not to get pregnant. (I learned.) She also translated for me the common obscenities, so at school I never appeared childish. How to write cheques for domestic bills and keep records—other pals taught me that, and to buy sanitary napkins on sale, close the door on salespeople, choose a dry-cleaner.

Like Mum, F assumed my homework was done, but when he saw my April report he didn't sign it automatically.

"Not good enough, Eleanor."

Did he imagine I could concentrate? I wept.

"I know." A pat. "Next term you'll do better."

Thus my mother's functions were distributed, except romance and sex. Hence, symbolically, the dinner date?

Does Murray's still exist?

Was it next day I left school illicitly for the first time?

My brain, reviving, observed that Wednesday's timetable would allow me, if I walked fast, to spend an hour at home by myself.

No. Not alone, for Mum filled each cubic inch. I heard her in the kitchen, I did, and ran to meet vacancy. A sound in her bedroom—rushed upstairs. Cried my face raw. Almost late to physics.

The next week, opening a drawer to meet a tangle of underwear and nightgowns, I felt dizzy. Banged that drawer back. Another, of heaped cardigans, sweaters, redolent of her. The jumbled dresses in her closet, same. I fled to school.

The next week, I held Mum's clothes against my body.

The next, addicted, I put them on. Buttoned, zipped. Through tweed jersey cotton I inhaled her perspiration.

Tried her lipsticks, cold cream, powder, Floris. Scrubbed (but my deskmate still sniffed).

On Mum's closet shelf, amid summer hats and shoes, lay used sewing patterns from McCalls, Simplicity. She'd filed F's letters, his notes really, between the crisp sepia sheets. He'd used business memo pads. In his large clear script, a few words filled a page.

Specialized Office Systems *I love you passionately*
Specialized Office Systems *Your skin thrills me*
Specialized Office Systems *I want you*. Again, again. *I need you more. Why cold, why? I love you so*. Below, SOS addresses and phone numbers in Toronto (head office), Hamilton, Ottawa.

I phoned my school. Truly, I felt unwell. My period had come, the first since Mum's death. Not long before, she'd tried again to talk about the m-word, about how, like me, she'd had irregular periods until what? No, loathsome, I turned my back. Did her menses stabilize post-childbirth? Several of my friends have described that phenomenon.

Over successive visits I peeked at those notes, fast, like testing a too-hot bath. *Please my darling, let me try*. Why kept? Stupid. *Much love*.

Did Mum reply?

Like her room and mine, F's contained desk bookcases dresser bed. Familiar, our three separate spaces. Puzzling, of late, the queries scarcely formulated.

F's closet held suits and shirts (pockets empty), and a tall shoe tree (shoes ditto). In his dresser lay socks now rolled into pairs by me, handkerchiefs ironed by me,

underwear folded by me with distaste. In upper drawers, ties. Cuff-links. Science medals from high school,
university.

Further search: illegal. *Don't touch F's desk!* Bare
wood but for inkwell, blotter, pen-holder, calendar. Three
drawers on each side. At right angles, a typing-table with
his IBM electric. <u>SOS</u> letterhead, carbons, and yellow
copy-paper lay in stacked metal trays.

My heart skittered. Must I wait till he, too, died?

I left the room.

Seven days later my anxiety morphed to eagerness as I
walked hastily from school to our house, but as I entered I
knew F was there—and he'd have heard the door.

Red-eyed, he came into the hall. "So you do this too."

We sat on the pine chest containing all our winter
boots, my old sled, F's snow-shovel, Mum's yardstick
for whacking icicles off the windowsills. Those swords
threatened her tulip bulbs.

Did he imagine I'd speak?

After a while F said, "The quiet feels as though she's
inside it."

Time went by.

I got up. "I have to go back to school."

"And I to work."

We went. My visits ended. Did F's? Did he hold her,
smell her? Did he locate his letters?

At term's end, no longer entitled to the privileges of
grief, I wrote exams with my class, and over the break
stayed with Aunt Kay while F attended an IBM conven-
tion. I'd hoped to search his desk. Instead, my aunt taught

me how to plan menus and budget. We spent hours at market. In her small kitchen I learned about stocks and soups, mastered cheese soufflé and plain sponge cake.

"Why Lucy put up with his food nonsense I never knew. She put up with a lot. That cream's not stiff enough, Eleanor."

To hear Mum's name just *spoken*, after months of sickening low tones, of pity-filled pawings at my shoulder—O gratitude! We cooked, laughed, cried, and Aunt Kay told me about Mr B's weekly visits. Astonishing.

"He loves good food too."

Married, of course.

I wasn't glad to see F again. Or sorry. He was just there, when I returned. Was that why Mum's presence/absence weighed less than I'd feared? Still, when F went out to a meeting or a business dinner, I only felt alone.

The new term's schedule offered chances to go home. Not just because F might be there, I didn't. Things were shifting. Tears exploded when Mum's sunglasses turned up, when I found her scrawled edits on *J of C*'s cornbread recipe, but otherwise I cried less. Crying took so long to stop, hurt too much.

In the summer, the pals overrode F's resistance and came to "deal with" Mum's clothes. (He left the house.) To help, I emptied her closet. The sewing patterns no longer held F's memos. A lurch—then a settling. I didn't want to reread them, or find what she wrote back.

My mother died at forty. Today, that's half the life-expectancy of a white woman in an industrialized country.

At forty I'd become assistant editor of the textbooks division, knew I'd likely have the big job in a few years.

That felt good. My one deaf-ish ear wasn't much of a problem.

Why did Mum feel her end was near? Didn't she enjoy her job? I checked. She'd won every sales award available to a part-timer. Did she plan full-time, after I'd graduated?

What about her and F? At home as a child, a young girl, I'd gone to sleep to the downstairs rhythm of their talk and amusement. At what? From the convertible's back seat, I saw my parents' heads turn. Inaudibly they exclaimed, smiled, pointed. Myself, I have not accepted the opportunities that came my way. If I'd had a big sister or been one, what might have changed?

Mum's death-year continued to form its circle. At school in the autumn I couldn't get out of typing class; Miss Whatsit thought it essential for modern women. F agreed.

"Your mother wasn't a touch typist. She taught herself, had her own odd fingering. You'll type faster than she ever could."

Aunt Kay steered us through Christmas towards February.

The prospect of the birthday sucked me deep down to grief again, though F and I, limpingly, were coping. My cooking improved, he ate more. I attempted tidiness, F noticed. He talked about <u>SOS</u> marketing plans, about the soon-to-be-released Selectric. I asked about proportional spacing. How could errors be corrected? He answered fully. Did such conversation offer him release?

When I complained about my dumb textbooks—"I could write better ones!"—he inspected them thoroughly,

"I agree, but Eleanor, right now good marks matter more."

Monthly we dined at Murray's, where F assumed a courtly manner with our regular waitress.

Two neighbours, elderly sisters, came for tea. I made Aunt Kay's scones, a success, and F walked the ladies home while I cleared up. How did he feel, finding only me when he got back? How was it to pass his Lucy's neat room, coverlet smooth, dresser and closet hollowed out? Her books remained. Did he, too, touch their pages?

Dread of the coming day swelled—and then F brought home tickets to Barnum and Bailey's.

"*The circus*, Dad?!"

Outrage. Refusal. Shouts. Tears.

Finally I heard him. "We need to get out of this. She'd love it."

Thus with a thousand other celebrants F and I gasped, laughed, screamed, clutched each other in the huge dark brilliant space of Mum's birthday,.

"Was I right?"

"Yes." We cried and laughed and cried again —

But no, we didn't.

No, for none of this happened.

Not a whit, because the parent who died abruptly when I was sixteen (not fifteen, not twelve) wasn't my mother.

Heart.

Mum's and Aunt Kay's, broken too.

Months later, I came home to a smoky smell. Mum stood at the sink, where heaps of torn paper smouldered into red, black. *Love,* I read. *Why not?* A tap trickled. Window wide, kitchen cold.

"Eleanor, you haven't finished packing your books."

With tongs Mum lifted scraps, fed air to her distinctive script, to his, till with a gobble the mass caught fire. *I can't be.* Splash, burn. *Lovely skin.*

"Did you hear me?"

"Yes."

We stood there till everything had drained away.

The house was for sale (Mum wasn't the listing agent). From our new apartment I'd ride the bus to school, but—*if* I got my license on my first try *and* acted more responsibly in general, *if*, then sometimes I could drive the Nash Rambler.

I got, I acted, I drove. At school, my status went up.

University neared.

I imagined that life, the life to follow. Would I win trophies?

At sixty-five, my mother died quickly of pancreatic cancer.

She'd told me long before how her periods regularized after my birth. How she envied Kay's big-sister capacity to contest F, and how lonely she was, widowed. Never anyone else. F's photo, B & W, 5 x 7, stood at her bedside. She kissed him good-night.

As her executor, while sorting Mum's chaotic papers I found that draft letter. *Strangely? Strongly?*

I emptied her dresser, laid things on her bed.

My very dear Aunt Kay chose first. (At Mr B's recent funeral, after decades of companionship, she'd been shunned.)

Then came the pals, to drink mournful wine and take a silk scarf, a brooch.

Once I'd queried Mum—that barn? the syrup? A head-shake. *No.*

Her safe-deposit box held a few photos. A gnarled man. Countrywomen in housedresses (do these now exist?), squinting at light.

I considered. In publishing, researchers abound. Hire someone? To what end? The dresser drawers suffice. I've now lived years longer than Mum did, yet I open hers and close them again. My father's, too. Some I thought full hold nothing now. Others contain things I never saw before.

FOOD

Edwin wore his red shoes. He brought the soup, our treat, and my choice this time. Oh the smell! Smoky Hungarian mushroom. Last month, we had my sister's winter favourite, roasted tomato. Our tastes never match, but come May we'll have a new menu. The war could be over by then. Basra's the news now.

As always, Edwin brought a chewy baguette, from the deli's own bakery. Eight chunks. Two thick curls of butter.

Our window sparkled with rain. We began.

A young woman, clutching a tiny child and a tote-bag, hurried towards us from the ladies' room. My sister smiled—but no, the mother targeted a bigger table nearby, where four people already sat.

From Seattle. We'd heard the older man grump about Vancouver's weather. Worse than home. And the border delay.

"Who're they kidding? Little toy country."

The mother placed her girl in a high chair at the table's end, near us. "Be good, Charlotte." A kiss. Then she sat, sighing, at the child's right. Pregnancy made her t-shirt ride up, rumpling its peace symbol and baring some belly. At the shirt's hem, a dry brown smear.

With a tissue she dabbed her cheeks and hairline.

The young man across from her asked, "What took so damn long, Ellie? I ordered for you."

Not awaiting a response, he resumed sotto-voce talk with the older woman next him. Angry? Yes. His mother? My sister and I, noting their similar features, agreed. Grandmother's hair shimmered blonde against a fitted black jacket. She sipped white wine.

To Ellie's right reared up a hefty male turtle-back. Grandfather? Must be. Evidently bored, he discussed US vs Canadian beer with a grey-haired woman at the table's far end. She, in a tracksuit, waving at the child, looked a coarser version of Grandmother. Great-aunt? We agreed.

We two sisters: our whole family. (Surprisingly common, that.) Our eyes speak to each other, our tiny gestures and lip movements refined over years.

As for Ellie's peace symbol, so public—such a luxury, to join in that struggle. I can't afford it, time, family, job. Since Shock-and-Awe, though, we've watched every newscast, every demo, to receive echoes of larger life and death.

Taking more bread, I add a scrape of butter. If I do that with three chunks, my last can be thick with yellow.

Ellie, ignored by her tablemates, smiled at her little one and kissed her nose. Charlotte yelped happily. When everyone looked, more yelps.

"Wants attention," said Grandmother.

"Who doesn't?" Great-aunt drained her beer, set down her empty amid glasses condiments cameras, took another. Grinning, the child waved her striped legs and bang-banged her Mary Janes against the high-chair.

"Nice stockings!" Great-aunt rose and lifted her pant-leg. "See? Red white blue."

"*Your* stripes aren't rainbow," said Grandmother. "Do *stop*, child."

My sister and I buy drugstore packs of Misty Beige pantyhose and knee-highs. Sometimes she wants a change and picks Cloud Grey, but it doesn't go with everything and she wants to borrow.

Empty-handed, Edwin hurried up—not to us. He whispered to the young dad, whose head snapped round to Ellie again.

"You left the damn stroller in the wrong place." Rising, "*I'll* deal with it."

"Hey you," cried Great-aunt. "Where's our food?"

Our spoons paused. *Hey?* Edwin, the deli's best waiter. Ours. He knows our schedule. For us he saves our two-table.

"Right away, ma'am."

Dad returned. "It's OK, Ellie, stop fussing."

Edwin returned. Soon Dad, Grandfather, Great-aunt forked up eggs, hot fish, cold cuts, yam fries, potato and pasta salads, coleslaw; freely they distributed salt ketchup hot-sauce mayo mustard pepper Thousand Island.

Grandmother's angry whispers didn't stop as she nibbled grapes, candied pecans, iceberg, nor did her son's.

Ellie cut foods on her plate into morsels. From the tote-bag came a plastic bowl, which she filled for Charlotte.

Who howled.

Turned red.

Stiffened.

Pressed herself against the high chair's tray, stuck her arms out. I knew my sister's hand would move toward the child. Did. With my right shoe's toe, I pressed her left foot. Hard. My sister withdrew, defeated. Thus we re-enacted a central scene in our history. To not tremble, I spooned up a whole fat delicious mushroom, filling my mouth.

"What the hell?" Grandfather, a yam fry in his left fist, reached straight across Ellie's chest towards Charlotte. "Here kid, they're great!"

The child slapped at the vegetable, screamed.

Grandmother smirked.

"Oh, your special spoon!" Ellie scrabbled in the tote. "Here, honey."

Charlotte quieted. With her fingers she ate efficiently, gripping the spoon upright in her other hand.

My sister smiled.

"Thank God." Grandfather ate fries.

Dad asked, "Ellie, why on earth not give her the spoon to begin with?"

On earth meant *the hell*, we knew.

"People do make mistakes. You didn't know that?"

Her sarcasm pleased us.

Dad turned again to his mother. We couldn't hear, and it's hard to lip-read sideways, but explosion felt close. The US did a long, angry hissing intro before it blew up

Iraq, and an amphibious landing now targets tiny Basra. Powerful, that word *amphibious*, near-magical: boats that crawl on land. Twenty years ago, Grenada got the amphibious treatment.

Ellie chewed and swallowed just three times before the child knocked a macaroni elbow off her tray. Surprised, Charlotte looked down. Smiled, and dropped another elbow. Another.

"No no!" The mother bent, napkin in hand. "Big girls eat properly."

Giggling, Charlotte pushed her bowl to teeter on the tray's edge. Again, my sister's hand stretched out towards the child.

Incorrigible. For years I didn't understand that, thought our Mum exaggerated. My big sister in high school, so lively, pretty, popular! On family trips to the beach, she helped me build sandcastles way taller than I could do alone. Once, though, she went away for months, had to repeat a grade.

Now Ellie's "No!" alerted Dad. He echoed her loudly. Too late. A big splat. Charlotte giggled. Table talk ceased as Ellie and Edwin scooped, wiped.

Dad frowned. "Bad girl!"

"So boring for her," said Great-aunt. "To sit still, with old people."

"She has to learn. Has to be *taught*." Glaring at Ellie. Who sat down again.

The men had almost cleared their plates. Grandfather, again reaching across Ellie, offered the child his last fries. She beamed, grabbed, ate.

"Thatta girl!" He took another beer, then appeared to notice the young woman beside him. "Did you want anything to drink?"

Ellie shook her head, refilling Charlotte's bowl.

Dad and Grandmother's whispers competed.

My sister and I don't raise our voices. In a small apartment, noise reverberates, and even quiet anger leaches into furniture, walls. Years later, words still resound. At home I never sit in the green chair where she once sat.

In my sister's twenties, little change occurred. Mum's summary, *Your sister has poor taste in men,* not only understated the case but also omitted alcohol, job losses, thieving, weight gain. We girls still lived at home, in my case to save money for school. Would a boy have got out?

As for my sister, she departed forever, came back, left *really* forever, returned broken. Etc., etc., well into her thirties. We'd enter the apartment to hear a particular silence. Gone again. Thus my taking care began, though our parents were then still fairly functional.

Great-aunt sighed, rose. "Jee-zus, this goddam family. Smoke break." Abandoning the half-eaten mush on her plate, she exited the deli to walk about under its awning, out of the rain.

I'd never leave my sister so, in public. After our monthly treat we always visit the ladies' room together.

"You girls don't eat. Look at that!" Grandfather pointed to Grandmother's salad, near-intact.

"I keep trim," she said. "Unlike some."

A flush started at Ellie's nape. Firmly she said, "Eat up, Charlotte!" Child and Great-aunt grinned, waving through the window.

Grandfather glanced at Ellie's plate, still heaped. "You don't eat either?"

Great-aunt blew a smoke-ring towards Charlotte and moved off to a corner newsstand to examine headlines. The child, abandoned, gazed with dislike at her bowl. Her face puckered. She squirmed, made the high chair rock.

"Stay still!" ordered Dad.

Two pieces of our bread remained. I still had most of my butter, my sister very little. Her eyes pleaded.

I wouldn't. Why should I? She could have done as I did, saved her butter, got through school to a decent job. I'm fifty-two. She's fifty-seven, done with menopause, but always I arrange with a staff person to phone me at once if she shows interest in any man. No call, for three years. Still I can't say that's over.

Dad said, "Stop wriggling!"

"She can't." Ellie took Charlotte from the high chair and set her on the floor by the tote bag. "See? She'll be just here, between us."

Grandmother asked, "Is that wise?"

Delighted, Charlotte explored the bag. She gnawed a tin of diaper cream, a tube of sunscreen, breathed hard while working at a small ziplock.

Ellie ate hungrily.

We rubbed our bowls clean. Soup and bread: a solid meal.

We enjoy, also, being out together. We enjoy people-watching. Our deli's far enough from home that we pass store windows we don't often see, also some not very familiar apartments and offices, a park with a new fountain. I work for the city's recreation department; that sparkle pleases me. At stores selling TVs, if there's a newscast we watch a bit. Heading home, we stop at the video store.

Grandfather took another beer.

Dad's neck went red. He hissed at Grandmother, whose fuchsia-nailed forefinger chased candied pecans around her plate.

Great-aunt tossed her cigarette butt on a high arc into traffic.

Back inside on a drift of stale smoke, she declared, "Iraq, big mistake. Waste of men, waste of money. We don't need their damned oil."

Grandmother turned on her. "Treasonous! Just like him." Her voice cracked. "Has *she* infected you too?"

Grandfather's leather-clad shoulders rose in a shrug.

Great-aunt shook more ketchup on her cold food and dug in, as Edwin brought the dessert menu.

Dad cheesecake. Grandfather bread pudding. Great-aunt chocky ice cream. Grandmother and Ellie no thanks.

Edwin knows not to offer us sweets, though my sister longs to come here, just once, just for cake. Or a tart, with coffee. "A *real* treat." After one monthly lunch she may harp on this notion, yet next time not mention it. All depends on how her volunteer work has gone, her weekly group, her few hours of paid work at the dollar store.

First, our Dad's memory faltered.

Next, Mum's cancer diagnosis dictated *You can't leave*. I stayed, with three dependents all aboard my little ship of state. In response, my periods stopped. Short. Never to go again.

At last! On the floor, Charlotte's efforts with the ziplock succeeded. She shook out a squeeze bottle. It rolled away, she reached, and Edwin, passing by, set down one red Doc Marten right by her hand. Only we noticed.

Long ago, sitting in the fat, upholstered green chair, my sister said, "I'll leave the city. I wouldn't have it here."

"No. *No.*"

"I'm nearly forty. Won't you help me?"

I pointed to the closed door of our parents' room. "I can't do this alone." The seal on Mum's colostomy bag had failed again. Our father had no idea of that, of anything.

"Please? I've despaired. It's my last chance."

"How would you manage?" Sound blasted out of my throat. "You can't even support yourself!"

My sister leaned back. I left the room.

Now Charlotte noticed, nearby, a pair of stilettos with twinkly ankle-bows. As she crawled, smiling, Edwin's shoe got her in the ribs.

Howls. Apologies. Dad retrieved her. "Why can't you watch her, Ellie?"

"All you've done is stuff your face and talk to *her!*"

Dad stroked Charlotte's curls. Ellie leaned fondly towards her, again exposing her own belly.

Grandmother hissed, "Diss-guss-ting."

"Hunh?" Grandfather.

"She doesn't even know she's shitty."

Great-aunt rose. "Would Charlotte let me hold her?"

No, but the child calmed.

"All this crap on the floor," Dad said.

"I'll clean it up."

"No, I will."

"She's quieting with you, goddammit! Stay with her."

The hiccuping girl clung to daddy.

Long ago, leaning back in the green chair, my sister sat, defeated.

Coping with bowels and bag took me fifteen minutes. When I returned to the living room, she'd gone to attempt a landing somewhere else.

Ten times over, a hundred, our father accepted whatever tale I told about repelling the invader. Months later, absent her amphibian, my sister reappeared. Mum was glad to have her older girl safe, or at least safer, at home, and didn't live to witness the worst breakdowns. I couldn't afford one of those.

Desserts arrived.

Charlotte wanted Dad's cheesecake, and got spoonfuls, giggling. Of course she had no idea what would happen to her entire life when Ellie's belly flattened.

After our Mum went, Dad lingered for a while.

As another while passed, I got my sister into treatment programs. Failure, repeatedly. More therapy, quiet routines. Slowly she grew able to volunteer, to step beyond the apartment where we live still. I don't step much further. Not till '94, decades after Vietnam, did the *DSM* define PTSD. Is that what we have? The boys at Basra will, for sure.

Grandmother looked at kneeling Ellie. "Aren't you

done *yet?*"

"Don't trouble yourself!"

But the older woman got off her chair. We dropped our napkins, leaned down to see Grandmother snatch, scratch at the stained t-shirt.

Ellie spat in her face.

Curses. Cries. A head struck the table's underside, and the deli filled with the public silence that advertises private scenes.

When Dad spoke into Grandmother's ear, she wept.

"Told you so." Grandfather scraped up Bourbon sauce. "Told you!"

Then Dad, still holding Charlotte, helped Ellie, his wife, to stand. He kissed her firmly and went to fetch the stroller.

The deli began talking again.

Charlotte, as Grandfather paid, watched the card-reader. She'd not ever noticed us. Near the deli's door, she waved her rainbow legs at Edwin, whose red Doc Martens did a quick soft-shoe for her.

I turned, smiling, to my sister. "How sweet!"

She wasn't there. Didn't see Charlotte depart at the prow of her family, older generations in her wake. Always new little girls arrive in the world, wee dears whose mum and dad adore them so they stay on and on with those who love and need them so, and they either don't grow up or turn into old women before they can vote. When my sister rose from that chair, she was nearly forty. Her child's father, who knows? She didn't.

What now? Go out in the rain to scan headlines about

murderous creatures grinding over sand. Run to the empty ladies', vomit mushrooms. Pay our bill, head for home. Perhaps I'd find my sister as I had before in public places, crying on a stranger's shoulder.

I managed a larger tip than usual. The rain, over. Everything shone. On the screens at the TV store, Basra's oil flamed.

She caught me up as I turned on to our street. Her smile, her arm about me, her warm hug: better than any food.

"That was just as good as TV!"

We giggled. Yes, we love our costume dramas. A Civil War series just finished, and there's a British mini on the Tudors. Terrifying, the Armada scenes.

SUMMER BOY

Standing in the guest room, Colin looked about. "Why are you making such a fuss?"

"Clean sheets, flowers, a fuss?" Amelia put her arms akimbo.

"Teenage boys don't notice things like that."

"Can't you smell it? Philadelphus. Lovely fragrance."

"He's got this bed for three weeks. Free. Isn't that enough?"

"He's your relative, not mine. And he has a name. Tobias." She began to cough, got water from the guest bathroom as Colin waited.

"I've never met him, nor do I want to. For good reason, I put those people behind me long ago."

"Tobias isn't to blame for his family. He's young, artistic. We're helping him."

"You didn't include me in deciding to do so."

Amelia flicked a grey hair from the shoulder of his jacket. Then she tested the bedside lamp, arranged some art magazines on the night table.

Colin went downstairs and out, to smoke a cigar and weed his herb garden. The low brick wall and box hedge—rosy red, deep green—set off the plantings, defined their place on a dark ground.

A dumpy English teenager in black, unsmiling. Fair hair. A duffle. Smeared glasses that guarded eyes hesitant to meet others. Headphones. In the car, silent all the way from the airport.

"Can't he utter?"

"You were shy once." Amelia looked over the herb garden. "Where's the tarragon?"

"Not doing well. Next year I'll try another variety." Colin held the kitchen door open. "I wasn't rude like him."

She came back in, holding her green handful. "What with your teaching and his classes, you'll hardly see Tobias. And I wish you'd let me get that jacket dry-cleaned. It reeks of cigar."

In a dense, silent mist, Tobias and Amelia rode the mini-ferry over False Creek to the art school. The grey silky water lapped, slipped by. When an invisible gull's screech startled all the passengers, the boy turned, smiling, to her. Together they found their way to the ceramics studio and met the famous Salvadorean potter.

On the return crossing, sunshine flashed on the creek, made the glass high-rises crackle with light. Dragon boats scissored through the blue.

How all this started:

In early spring, Amelia answered the phone.

"Colin's not home just now. Who? Would you repeat that please? England? Cousin? My goodness, hello! Twice removed. London? Oh Basingstoke. Removed, so confusing. No, Colin doesn't say much about you. Who? Ceramics, at Emily Carr? Your grandson must be good, to be admitted to a master class! Yes, we're close to Granville Island, excuse me, oh it's just bronchial. Three weeks? Delightful. What's your email?" Etc.

"Can't that boy shut up sometimes?"

"Tobias is feeling more at home."

Colin grimaced. "Pretentious Oxbridge accent."

"You had that too."

"How can you watch that silly show with him?"

"It makes us laugh. Colin, you look as sour as Henry James!"

What Colin did say about England, when he met Amelia:

"I was orphaned. That old bitch quote *took me in*. Convinced me I was useless. Stupid. They all agreed. Emigrating, I put them behind me."

In Canada, his specialty became American literature, and he lived in his own private country of lecturing, writing.

When Amelia quit graduate work in French literature to teach high school, Colin said, "*Do what you want*. You're the first person who ever told me that." When she quit teenagers in favour of Montessori, he said it again.

Amelia's country: a workroom full of bright clear colours, decisive shapes. No ambiguity. The kids, like good candy and furniture, tested solid all through. From the moment they arrived she was well-used, but they always left so soon. Leaving leaving leaving.

Tobias enjoyed picking herbs, running the food processor, shaping ground beef into patties stuffed with Roquefort for the barbecue. Efficiently he filled and emptied the dishwasher.

"Tobias says his family has a cook."

"So he could have stayed in a hotel. Cheapskates. Using me, still."

"Must you be so negative? Tobias could be our grandson."

"Thank God he isn't." A breath. "I'm sorry, Amelia."

"Not very."

"I said *I'm sorry*. Still, you had no right to redesign my life."

"I heard you." Amelia coughed. "So I can't have a child even for twenty-one days?"

"You spend five days a week with children."

"Not where I live."

"But *I* live here."

"It's good to come home to young life. Wake up to it." She took a lozenge from a jar. "Who's forever saying *I put all that behind me?* Get real. Life's tapping at your shoulder."

"Is your bronchial stuff getting worse?"

"It isn't *stuff*. Not like a lipstick or keys."

"Amelia, every winter when your chest's bad and you have to rest so much, I miss you."

The lozenge smelled lemony. "Even a pretend grandson means we're getting old, Colin. A wake-up call."

"I'm nowhere near retiring."

"Ten, give or take. Can't you hear the years passing?"

"How much longer is this boy to be with us?"

"Look at the calendar." Amelia filled a pie shell with fruit.

"Another week."

"The award ceremony's on the last day. He's done good work."

"Pots."

She poured custard over top. "*Ceramics* is the word you want."

"*Pattern* is, actually. You're so impulsive, Amelia. Postgraduate, high school, Montessori, chopping, changing."

"You encouraged me!"

"Now this boy."

She shoved the pie into the oven, stood tall. "Tobias is equivalent?"

"Next you'll jump down to infants, be a midwife." He took a stray raspberry from the counter and ate it.

After her cough settled she said, "We've both grown in ways I didn't expect. Like seeds that turn out different from the package."

"I haven't changed." Colin located another raspberry.

"Exactly." She took bowls and beaters to the sink. "This isn't rock paper scissors, your pain beats mine.

If Tobias had no family connection, would you feel different?"

He followed her, to lick the beaters. "I don't want anyone but you."

Colin sat reading, while Amelia filled in a crossword and imagined the deliverance of babies. Compelling. She was perhaps not too old to retrain? Stillbirths, though— unbearable. Eight Across was *raven*, who stole the sun. Her children adored that story, laughing as they leapt out of cardboard boxes to wave yellow felt circles in the air.

From upstairs Tobias shouted, "Amelia, come see!"

She rose.

"You're not that boy's servant. Sit down!"

Up the stairs, quick step step step on shining wood. Then carpet, then exclamations. Down again, fast, eager.

"Colin, you're pouting like Churchill when Karsh took his cigar."

He held his book as if about to throw it. "You wouldn't jump up for me. You wouldn't run upstairs."

"We don't shout."

"Exactly." He started towards his study. "I have essays to mark."

Amelia called after him, "Tobias got an A on his major project. He's going to be a potter."

Of course the door closed. Thirty years.

When they retired, would she be his child at last?

Colin and Amelia en route from the airport, as Tobias soared over the Pole towards Basingstoke:

"I've told you, I don't want him—

"Tobias."

—here next summer. Amelia, you never had to live with strangers."

"No?"

He groaned. "That again?"

"You knew I wanted them. You never said you didn't. Not a word."

"I described my childhood. I told you what I'd been through."

"And I've paid for it." She coughed. "He'll come for six weeks, next summer."

"Are you crying?"

"Do you see tears?"

In December, Amelia noticed that a mole on Colin's inner thigh looked different. At once she made the appointment, and later emailed Basingstoke: "Next summer's visit is in doubt."

Then the couple set out across the harsh terrain of biopsy, preliminary diagnosis, diagnosis, sick leave, chemotherapy, radiation, effects, side effects, observation, reassessment. Colin noted, pleased, that the Anglo-Saxon *sick* stood almost alone.

"The core of the experience." He quit smoking.

Every night the couple dreamed hugely, of lakes with silver ice crumpling on the shore, of hard wood forests in autumn, of bridges that terminated in fog. They saw a library burn. They held goblets of their own blood, crystallized, sparkling. Their long-deceased parents sported furry rabbit ears and hopped about on the snow, lippety-lip.

Amelia and Colin woke early each day. They began by telling each other what had happened in the dark, and cuddled while the tapestries floated about their bedroom, became transparent, dislimned.

"So nice that our pillows don't smell of smoke any more."

"Did they?"

The couple rose when Amelia had to eat and get to work. Afterwards Colin often slept again, but those richly embroidered visions didn't come.

The winter rains ended, the April rains began.

With vigour Amelia did the spring clean-up in her flower beds.

"Don't touch the herb garden," Colin said. "I'll get to it." He didn't. Groundsel and a not-useful kind of dandelion grew thick.

All over the city, cherry trees bloomed, fairy-tale white or Wife-of-Bath pink. Amelia sighed. "Aren't you sorry we never planted one?"

"But the heavy shade! That's why we agreed not to."

"I know."

"All your flowers are fragrant. That's what you said you wanted."

In early May, Colin's doctor chuckled. She thumped her patient on the back and cried, "Get out of here!" He stood silent, tears sliding down.

At home, getting out of the car, he blurted, "Amelia, this time together—unforgettable. Like the beginning."

That evening she checked the art school's website. Only a few days remained to confirm attendance at July's summer school.

She emailed Basingstoke.

"I can't believe you didn't cancel that boy."

"You can't punish Tobias for a few bad years."

"Five. A long time for a teenager."

She coughed. "One-eleventh of your life."

"Time's different when you're young."

"Indeed."

"Why don't you see the doctor about your throat?"

Amelia giggled. "When I'm old I'll just be like my mum, with a shot glass of cherry cough syrup by the bed. Spiked."

Tobias was taller, thinner. Carried a bigger duffle. Wore contacts.

"I'll arrange my room," he told Amelia. "I've planned it all. Could you take those flowers away? They smell too strong."

He did not want to whip egg whites or to laugh at Poirot. The gondola up Grouse was rejected, also a trip to Victoria, and Tobias took the ferry across the Creek alone, to register at the school.

Unimpressed by the raku specialist from Prague, after classes he lingered for hours with the other students, allegedly to drink coffee.

"I wish he'd call to let me know," said Amelia. For the third night in a row she and Colin were eating alone on the back porch. Nearby, the nicotiana released its scent.

"Your boy's becoming independent."

"Thoughtless."

Colin smiled. He took seconds of salmon and asparagus.

Amelia hadn't bothered to ice the cake she'd made for dessert. When Tobias, returning, became querulous about this, she pointed to the fridge. He located chocolate sauce, drenched a hunk of cake, gobbled. Then he went outside, where Colin was nipping vaguely at weeds.

She called through the screen door, "Dishwasher!"

First he took more cake. Afterwards he helped Colin clear the beds, working on and on till the dusk became too deep.

The next night he was on time for dinner, lively and talkative, praising the Caesar, emptying the bowl. Several times he mentioned the name *Melanie*. Afterwards he cleared and loaded without being asked, took out the garbage.

Amelia, putting food away, glanced out the kitchen window.

Colin, smiling, handed Tobias a cigar and the two lit up. The red tips glowed. Before she could shout, her cough began. Companionably, the boy waved his cigar at the man. Then he turned away, trotted alongside the house and out of view.

ACKNOWLEDGMENTS

My thanks to

the editors of *Fiddlehead*, *Joyland*, *The Malahat Review*, *The New Quarterly*, *Numero Cinq*, and *Room Of One's Own*, where some of these stories originally appeared

John Metcalf, my editor

Dan Wells, my publisher, and all the staff at Biblioasis for their excellent work

and Dean, my partner, *sine qua non*

ABOUT THE AUTHOR

Cynthia Flood's most recent book, *Red Girl Rat Boy* (Biblioasis 2013), was shortlisted for the BC Book Prizes' fiction award and long-listed for the Frank O'Connor award, besides appearing on "best of year" lists for *Quill & Quire* and *January Magazine*. Earlier collections are *The English Stories* (Biblioasis 2009), *My Father Took a Cake to France,* and *The Animals in their Elements.* Her work has been selected six times for *Best Canadian Stories,* and appears often in both print and online literary magazines. She lives in Vancouver's West End.